Praise

MW00966534

"Pauline Carelli-Bloom, budding novelist, is not only charming, she's also winning, captivating and irresistible!"
— Susan Juby, author of *Alice, I Think*

"This is a funny one. It will leave you, as Pauline might say, ROFL."
— *Quill & Quire*

"Ravel's touch is light but spot on; the prospect of a series … is good news for young adult readers."
— *Globe and Mail*

"Pauline has an off-centre take on the world. Her narrative is rich with delightful one-liners and not one of them is generic."
— *Quill & Quire*

"… filled with friendship foibles, goofups with boys, parental antics and general mayhem."
— *Edmonton Sun*

"… a fast and easy read … read all the books in the series."
— *Kidzworld*

Check out the other titles in the Pauline, btw series!

The Thrilling Life of
Pauline de Lammermoor
978-1-55192-988-0
$11.95

The Mysterious Adventures of
Pauline Bovary
978-1-55192-986-6
$11.95

The Secret Journey of
Pauline Siddhartha
978-1-55192-974-3
$11.95

Have you had a chance to visit Pauline, Augusta and Leila's
online Gallery of Greatness? (It's pretty cool. There's art,
articles and even a poem about Kalan. That's right. Kalan!)
Check it out at **www.augustaplemarre.com/**

The Secret Journey of

Pauline
Siddhartha

Pauline, btw
BOOK THREE

The Secret Journey of
Pauline
Siddhartha

EDEET RAVEL

RAINCOAST BOOKS

Vancouver

NOTE: all translations of Hermann Hesse's work are the author's own.

Raincoast Books gratefully acknowledges the ongoing support of the Province
of British Columbia through the BC Arts Council and the Book Publishing
Tax Credit and the Government of Canada through the Canada Council for
the Arts, and the Book Publishing Industry Development Program (BPIDP).

Edited by Colin Thomas
Cover and interior design by Teresa Bubela
Typeset by Five Seventeen

Library and Archives Canada Cataloguing in Publication

Ravel, Edeet, 1955–
    The secret journey of Pauline Siddhartha / Edeet Ravel.

ISBN 13: 978-1-55192-974-3
ISBN 10: 1-55192-974-0

        I. Title.

PS8585.A8715S42 2007   jC813'.54   C2007-900488-1

Library of Congress Control Number: 2007921212

Raincoast Books   *In the United States:*
9050 Shaughnessy Street   Publishers Group West
Vancouver, British Columbia   1700 Fourth Street
Canada V6P 6E5   Berkeley, California
www.raincoast.com   94710

Raincoast Books is committed to protecting the environment and to the
responsible use of natural resources. We are working with suppliers and printers
to phase out our use of paper produced from ancient forests. This book is
printed with vegetable-based inks on 100% ancient-forest-free, 40% post-
consumer recycled, processed chlorine- and acid-free paper. For further
information, visit our website at www.raincoast.com/publishing/.

Printed in Canada by Webcom.

10 9 8 7 6 5 4 3 2 1

Acknowledgements

When my daughter Larissa was much younger, I read the books she was reading (often because I was reading out loud to her) and those books inspired me to create the Pauline series. Larissa was my first editor. She set me in the right direction, and it is no exaggeration to say that Pauline wouldn't have got past the first page of her novel without the expert advice of Larissa (who's much better at it than Zane). Thank you, sweetie!

I am grateful to all the folks at Raincoast, who did such an amazing job producing these books. I love the way they came out. Thanks, guys.

I would like to thank my superb editors, Joan Deitch and Colin Thomas, and my wonderful friend and negotiator Cesar Garza.

I'm grateful to the friends who believed in my writing and encouraged me, and to my many students, who were my teachers as much as I was theirs. I remain eternally grateful to my first creative writing teacher, Terence Byrnes. He took me seriously as a writer, and saw potential in the not-very-good stories I handed in nearly twenty-five years ago.

I owe an apology to the great writer James Joyce, and his readers. I did not have permission to quote him, and the sentence attributed to him on page 99 is mine.

Lana Coviensky, to whom the second Pauline book is dedicated, died a day before the first Pauline manuscript arrived at her house, but at least she knew about the dedication, and it made her very happy. When I was Pauline's age, Lana — a childhood friend of my mother's — gave me loving attention with a generosity of spirit that can never be forgotten. The magical effects of kindness to young people can last a lifetime.

On the Acknowledgements page we only mention people who helped us — but everyone we encounter is part of our lives, and all our experiences, happy and sad, shape us and bring us to where we are now. The difficulties in our lives can give us insight and lead us to compassion, and they become an important part of our voyage. There is always kindness out there, when we are ready for it.

1

This is Pauline Carelli-Bloom, high school student and teen novelist.[1] I am picking up my pen once again, because yesterday my life changed. Yesterday I met the wise and handsome guru Nigel Sivananda. He has opened my eyes.

First, I'll tell you who I am. Zane Burbank III, author of *You Too Can Write a Great Novel!* warns: *Remember to tell your readers Where, Who, When, What and Why!* He says too many writers get right into their story without bothering to mention, for example, that it's in an African jungle — and then suddenly there's a lion in a story that you thought was in New York. Or else the writer forgets to tell readers that the story is about the Middle Ages, and suddenly there's someone being burned at the stake.

---

[1] My two previous novels, in case you want to read them, are *The Thrilling Life of Pauline de Lammermoor* and *The Mysterious Adventures of Pauline Bovary.*

So, to avoid confusion, here is the basic information you need to know:

Where: Ghent, which is a small town in Ontario, Canada, except that right now — I still can't believe it! — I'm in London, England, visiting my grandmother for the Christmas break.

Who: The main characters in this novel are:

1. Me, Pauline, aged almost fifteen (fourteen days to go!).

2. My parents. They're divorced but Seeing Other People. Dad's seeing an old woman called Bunny — she's fifty-six — and Mom is seeing a short but nice man from Greece called Agatone, which is pronounced like "rigatoni."

3. My friends: Genevieve (a figure skater), Yoshi (my boyfriend), Rachel (lives with religious grandmother), Leila (recently getting wild), Naomi (new high-school friend), Chad (a genius, also new) and sometimes Augusta (the girl who has everything).

4. My grandmother Daphne. I'm in her "flat" (apartment) as I write!

5.   Nigel Sivananda, whom I met yesterday.
     He has changed my life.

When: The present.

What: The main topic of my novels is my life,
          because, as Zane advises in one of his Basic
          Rules, *Write about what you know best.*

Why: Because "Truth is always exciting" (Pearl S.
          Buck).

Zane says not to make chapters too long, and
Daphne, my grandmother, is calling me for breakfast,
so I will continue with Chapter 2 later.

2

I have just had a delicious breakfast of four toasted crumpets — two with honey and the others with an interesting spread called Marmite. I know that sounds like something made with insects, but it's actually quite tasty.

Crumpets, in case you have never been to this part of the world, are small round buns with lots of little holes on top. When you spread butter on a hot toasted crumpet, it goes right into the holes and dribbles over everything, including your chin, so it takes a bit of practice to eat it without making a mess. It's worth the effort, however. The contrast between the salty, flavourful Marmite and the heavenly sweet honey is an experience not to be missed.

As I ate and sipped "a nice cup of tea" — as my grandmother put it — the weak winter sun poured in on the tiny kitchen table from a tiny window. The kitchen doesn't have cupboards, only shelves, and all the dishes and boxes of food are on the shelves. Very exotic. The fridge is also extremely cute. It's a mini-fridge that fits under the counter. I remember that fridge from when I was five years old and my parents dropped me off at Daphne's before they went travelling through Europe and Asia. The mini-fridge was a hungry child's dream come true — all you had to do was open the door and reach in.

And here I am again! Back in the incredible and breathtaking city of London, England. I was not in a position to appreciate London when I was a pre-schooler.

In the first chapter, I told you I was taking up my pen once more. Ordinarily, that would be a metaphor meaning, "I'm writing," but this time I really am using a pen, because Daphne's computer has been invaded by a virus of an unseemly and shocking nature. The virus consists of non-stop, flashing images, but if I described these images, my book would be rated X, which is not recommended by Zane Burbank III. He advises writers: *Try to reach as wide an audience as possible.*

I'd be too embarrassed to describe the virus anyhow. It was bad enough having to call Daphne when the virus suddenly appeared as I was checking my e-mail this morning. I left the room, of course, but I could hear Daphne sighing as she tried to reboot.

My poor grandmother! She has probably never seen such things before.

I'm trying to get used to calling my grandmother "Daphne." She doesn't like words like "Gran" or "Grandma" because she says they are "a demeaning attempt to marginalize anyone who can't sell shampoo on telly (TV) by virtue of being eighteen years old." Daphne says we live in a lookist, sexist, ageist and specist society. A specist is someone who thinks the human species is superior to other species, like whales and stray dogs. I personally think we are superior to some other species, like mosquitoes, for example, or carpenter ants. But I didn't say anything, because I didn't want to seem unfeeling. To find out about my horrific encounter with carpenter ants, you will have to read my previous novel, *The Mysterious Adventures of Pauline Bovary*.

This is my second day in London. I arrived by plane at Heathrow Airport yesterday, at three o'clock in the afternoon. It was my first time on a plane alone. In fact, it was my first time travelling by *any* vehicle alone (not counting my bike). When Dad booked my ticket, they asked him if he wanted to pay extra for me to be watched over. Dad said, "No, thanks. I have full confidence in my daughter's ability to get on and off the plane by herself without a major mishap." That's a pretty long sentence for my dad. He's not usually a talkative person.

Actually, the experience of flying to London was not exactly joyful. For those of you who have not read my previous novels, I have to inform you that I once had a truly traumatic experience in an airplane. My dad's friend Bunny took me and Dad up in her toy airplane and we almost had a fatal crash. I have looked death in the face, and "Death is a fearful thing" (W. Shakespeare, *Measure for Measure*).

I'll describe my difficult transatlantic flight in the next chapter.

3

I'm impatient to tell you about Nigel Sivananda, so I hope you don't mind if I summarize my difficult transatlantic flight briefly.

To make a long story of severe suffering short, as soon as we were up in the air, I realized that only a piece of metal separated me from the vast, empty sky, and I also realized that if this piece of metal suddenly came apart, I would have nothing to hold on to as I fell helplessly through the void to my certain death. I don't know why they don't equip passengers with parachutes, in case of emergency.

Had Nigel Sivananda been with me, he would have immediately moved my chakras and brought me peace and serenity. We could have chanted together during the entire flight.

Luckily, the woman sitting next to me was very nice, which is the next best thing to being enlightened. She noticed my trembling body, my pale face, my help-less moans and the way I was clutching the armrest between us. She gave me some Swiss chocolate and told me she had twenty-four grandchildren. She revealed that she was a Mormon. I don't know what a Mormon is, exactly, but they seem to be a very friendly sort of people.

I told her I was a novelist, and she asked with great interest about my accomplishments. So I described my first two novels, *The Thrilling Life of Pauline de Lammermoor* and *The Mysterious Adventures of Pauline Bovary*, in detail. I covered most of my plots: my parents' divorce (conflict), my best friend Genevieve's secret friend (mystery), how I almost lost my boyfriend Yoshi (more conflict), how Genevieve went to Toronto to study figure skating for the Olympics (loss and sadness), how both my parents became involved with new people (change and upheaval), and so on. My neighbour made little sounds with her throat, to show that she was paying keen attention, even though her eyes kept darting around in every direction.

Before I knew it, it was time to eat from a little tray. My neighbour must have been quite hungry, as she gave a big sigh of relief.

My grandmother — I mean, Daphne — had ordered and paid for my ticket, so my meal was marked "vegan." That means it was made without animal products. The main dish was surprisingly good. It was some kind of rice in tomato sauce, sprinkled with sesame seeds and raisins. Not bad at all. I would have enjoyed a real dessert instead of the fruit salad. I eyed my neighbour's coconut cream cake longingly, I have to admit.

To my surprise, I fell asleep after I ate, and before I knew it, the Mormon woman was waking me up because we had to put our seatbelts back on. "You had a long sleep," she said cheerfully. "Good for you!"

However, as soon as I remembered that I was on a plane, my suffering returned to haunt me. "I see nothing with my eyes, and there's a drumming in my ears, and sweat pours down me, and trembling seizes all of me" (Sappho).

This time, the Mormon woman didn't try to engage me in conversation. She only said, "There, there, we'll soon be landing." I could tell the long flight had made her quite tired.

Without anyone to comfort and console me, I remained gripping my armrest in a state of terror, and no one on Earth was happier than I was when the wheels finally hit the ground.

I'm trying not to think about having to fly back to Canada at the end of my visit. Maybe by then I will have enough inner peace to overcome the earthly shackles of fear and dread.

4

I'm very glad *indeed* that I brought my thesaurus and my *Dictionary of Famous Quotations* on this trip. ("Indeed" is an extremely popular word here.)

A thesaurus is a book with many synonyms, and the *Dictionary of Famous Quotations* is a collection of profound and moving quotes throughout the ages. Most of the quotes are by men, I've noticed. This is probably because back in the old days, men were the ones who collected the quotes. They didn't bother including all the good things women said.

I didn't think I'd be working on a new novel during my vacation in London, but I feel that no novelist should travel without these indispensable guides. You never know when inspiration might strike you like a "bell within the steeple wild, The flying tidings told." (Emily Dickinson. Great metaphor, Emily!)

On the other hand, I didn't bring the most important book of all with me: *You Too Can Write a Great Novel!* by Zane Burbank III. That's because by now I pretty much know it by heart. I mean, I used it to guide me through two whole novels. I followed all the rules, took all the advice and applied the many excellent suggestions that Zane made. So at this point, you could say I'm an expert on Zane's book.

I admit that these two books, the thesaurus and the *Dictionary of Famous Quotations*, made my knapsack quite heavy. I had decided not to take a suitcase for the trip to London, because Dad said the best way to travel is to have as little luggage as possible.

"Just take whatever you can fit into a knapsack, Pauline. You can always buy what you're missing in London. Most people travel as if they were war refugees headed for the Sahara Desert," he said. That was also a fairly long speech for Dad. Since he met Bunny, he's become a bit more wordy.

He showed me his old backpack from his trip through Europe and Asia with Mom. It was dusty and somewhat raggedy, but Dad looked at it with admiration and longing. I guess it brought back memories of his long-gone youth.

Unfortunately, my two indispensable books took up most of the room in my knapsack. But, as Zane so truthfully points out, *A writer must make many sacrifices!*

It made me feel really cool to fly from Canada to London with only a knapsack. Anyone looking at me in the airport could easily get the impression that I constantly go back and forth from one country to the other, without a moment's thought — like my occasional friend and classmate Augusta. Augusta does take luggage, however. She needs suitcases for all the gifts she buys for herself in Mexico and other exotic locations.

Anyhow, thanks to Dad's advice, I didn't have to wait for my luggage when I got to Heathrow Airport. I went straight out through the sliding doors. Daphne was waiting to meet me with a bunch of blue wildflowers. She was wearing jeans, a short denim jacket and Timberland boots. She doesn't dress like a grandmother.

"Pauline! How lovely to see you! Look at you — you've become a teenager!"

The last time Daphne saw me I was still sucking my thumb.

"You're already taller than your mother. Taller than me, too," she said approvingly.

"I've always been on the tall side," I explained modestly. I measured myself in gym class a few weeks ago, and I'm five feet, eight-and-three-quarters inches tall, though I still don't have boobs.

Daphne was quite impressed that I only brought one knapsack. "I'm glad to see you like travelling light," she said. "Now — how was your flight?"

"The part where I was sleeping was fine," I said, my voice still unsteady. "Thanks for the pretty flowers, Daphne."

Daphne has a tiny little car, with the driver's seat on the wrong side. That's how cars are made here, with the driver sitting where the passenger is supposed to be, and vice versa. It's very strange, but that's the way they accidentally built their first cars long ago, and now they're stuck with the mix-up. How unfortunate for them!

Daphne doesn't have an English accent, but she's the exception. Oh, I wish I had one of the accents I heard in the airport! They're all so beautiful. They make everyone sound so smart and interesting and polite. Canadian pronunciation is really boring in comparison. I'd take the mixed-up cars any day, as long as I got the accent with them!

Even though she doesn't have an accent, Daphne uses British words, like "telly" for TV and "flat" for apartment. That's because she's lived in London for over twenty years. My mom always said I was too young for the story of how Daphne ended up in London. "When you're older, I'll tell you," she would say mysteriously. I'm sure I'm old enough now! What could shock me at this point? I am a child of the internet. Also, I watch *Dr. Phil*.

We are going out now, so I'll have to wait until tonight to reveal how my eyes were opened and my life was transformed.

5

I have just had an amazing day in the soul-searing city of London!

I would tell you about it right away, but Zane Burbank III repeatedly exhorts: *Go in chronological order! The days when publishers would read past the first two sentences of Finnegan's* Wake *are long gone.* I don't know who Finnegan was, but I guess his book *Wake* didn't follow this rule.

So, to continue from where I left off in Chapter 4, as soon as we got to Daphne's, she told me that she had invited some of her friends to come over in the evening so they could meet me. Daphne has a lot of energy, and she thinks everyone else does, too. But I didn't mind having a party right away: I was far too excited to go to sleep yet. And besides, I had that nap on the plane.

Daphne's flat is in North London. It was built for elves. I'll draw it for you at the end of this chapter, so you can get an idea of the layout. As you will see, it has a tiny kitchen, two tiny bedrooms on either side of a tiny living room, and a tiny bathroom with only enough room for a shower stall. My poor grandmother has had to give up baths for twenty years! When I expressed my sympathy, Daphne smiled pleasantly and said, "Most people on this planet don't even have clean drinking water, dear. I can survive without a bath. Besides, my friend Pedro has a bath, which is always at my disposal."

Another drawback to this flat is that the hallways of the building are out in the open, like long, endless balconies. As a result, Daphne's apartment is quite chilly. Well, freezing, really, even though it doesn't get as cold in London as it does in Canada, luckily. There aren't any thermostats, so I don't know exactly how cold it is. In the living room, Daphne has a small built-in heater that you light with matches. But basically you have to get used to wearing sweaters indoors. Daphne has also lent me a thermal undershirt.

To take a shower in a cold room, you must first turn the water on, then quickly undress and hop under the steaming water. I didn't figure this out until I was undressed. I then discovered that the knobs of Daphne's shower are broken, and as a result they're extremely difficult to turn on. I had to wrap my shivering body in a towel and call Daphne. She came into

the bathroom and turned the water on for me.
"Slightly chilly today, isn't it?" she commented. I
couldn't answer because my teeth were chattering, but
Daphne didn't notice. She's used to the harsh condi-
tions of her life.

In spite of these drawbacks, Daphne's rent is twice
what Mom pays for our luxury condo in Ontario! And
Daphne says she's very, very lucky, because this is a
"council flat," which means the owners are not allowed
to raise the rent as high as they'd like to. She says that
anywhere else, she'd be paying ten times as much.

"How come rents are so astronomical here?" I
queried.

"Because a great many people want to live in
London, dear. It's the law of supply and demand. The
more the demand, and the smaller the supply, the
higher the price."

Well, I can certainly understand why everyone
wants to live here. London is the most heart-thrilling,
soul-expanding, spirit-stirring and stimulating city in
the entire world. But I will get to that later. I don't
want to make the same mistake Finnegan made,
though I must say I'm curious about his book now. I'll
ask Daphne if she's ever heard of *Wake*.

I was excited about meeting my grandmother's
friends, but I was also a little worried. How would

everyone fit into the living room? Not only is it really small, but it's full of cardboard boxes that contain flyers and information about Problems of the World. Daphne spends a lot of time trying to solve the Problems of the World. Personally, I don't know how she manages to be in a good mood all the time, surrounded as she is by stories of misery and despair.

Each box is labelled with a different Problem. Whales. Child Slavery. Adult Slavery. Corporate Corruption (local). Corporate Corruption (global). Government Corruption (local). Government Corruption (global). You get the idea.

If I had to think about all the Problems of the World every single minute, I'd go stark raving mad. But Daphne likes thinking about them. "I know it's a drop in the ocean, but at least I'm trying," she remarked.

Before the guests arrived, Daphne and I put up some holiday decorations. The decorations were "non-denominational," in order to avoid giving one religion priority over others. Mostly they were variations on a winter theme. A cute snowflake mobile, little wooden people on sleds and streamers made of shiny gold and white paper. There were also stars on the window panes. It seems every religion goes in for stars. That must be because everyone sees them, everyone wonders about them, and everyone likes how they look up there in the vast, endless night sky.

Daphne gave me a list of the guests' names, so I would have some idea of who was coming. The names were very exotic: Amelia, Dermot, Baddi, Souad, Cyril, Patricia, Xisheng, Derek, Trevor, Antonia, Violaine, Radim, Siobhan (pronounced "ShiVON," good thing I found that out before the party) and Nigel. The friend with the bath, Pedro, couldn't make it. He was rehearsing for a play called, *The End of the World in Uncle Sham's Basement.*

Everyone arrived on time and the party went very well *indeed*. Daphne's friends sat on the floor with their backs against the Problem boxes. And even though in Canada it might have felt crowded, it didn't feel crowded here in London, because people here are geniuses at social situations. Everyone pretended that they were in a big, magnificent castle, and it worked! I mean, they acted as if they were extremely comfortable and sitting on velvet sofas, and you ended up believing that it was true.

They were also on the quiet side. They didn't all speak at once, the way we do. They waited their turn while politely sipping their tea. Oh, I wish I could live in such a civilized place!

Daphne's friends are all ages, from young to old. And they are from all walks of life. Some of her young friends work in factories and some of them go to famous universities. The ones who work in factories were dressed in really cool designer clothes, while the ones who go to famous universities were wearing old jeans, dirty running shoes and faded T-shirts.

They all treated me as if I was some famous, important person. Everyone asked me questions and included me in the conversation. This is probably a rule of politeness in the United Kingdom. Another rule is that when you say something, people don't just move on to another subject. First they comment in an approving way on what you said, usually by exclaiming "Brilliant!" I like these rules.

The other strange thing about the party was the food. There is a square table in the corner of the living room, and Daphne put a lot of lovely things on it: cakes and fruit and cheese and bread and olives and nuts. But everyone ignored the food, as if it didn't exist, instead of pouncing on it like we do at home.

They talked and drank tea for a whole hour before Daphne invited them to eat. But no one wanted to go first, so it was *another fifteen minutes* before people actually began to eat. And the only reason they started to eat was that I finally got desperate and took the initiative. I mean, I was starving. I couldn't just sit there and not eat any longer. So I got up and cut a slice of bread, covered it with cream cheese and bit in.

Slowly, one by one, Daphne's friends also got up and helped themselves to a little food, in a shy way. People here are shy about eating. They don't want to look like pigs.

Daphne would get mad at me for saying "like pigs." But it's just an expression. I don't mean to be insulting to pigs. However, pigs can't read or write, and they don't understand human language, so they will never know that people say mean things about them. Besides, it's perfectly fine to eat like a pig if you *are* a pig.

Once the trial of eating was out of the way, and a few bottles of wine had been opened, everyone was much more relaxed. They must have been quite stressed out about the food problem, and they were relieved when it was solved.

That was when I spoke to Nigel Sivananda. The guests got into little groups, and some wandered off to the kitchen, while others stood in the doorway to Daphne's bedroom or sat on Daphne's bed and looked at some posters they were working on. The guests looking at the posters belonged to the People's Equality Action Group. Or maybe I should say, they *were* the People's Equality Action Group. They were trying to decide whether to include their logo (a red flag), or to leave it out in order to draw in more people. Should they be proud of who they are, or should they be practical and simply omit it? It was a heated debate.

I wasn't all that interested in the discussion about the flag, and as the kitchen had five people squeezed into it, which is the maximum it can hold, I settled in the living room, next to the Victims of Torture box. That was when I found myself sitting next to Nigel Sivananda. We had a long, deeply enlightening conversation.

Nigel Sivananda has blue eyes that pierce your soul and penetrate your thoughts. He also has a sandy-coloured beard and he wears all-white clothes. This is because he is at peace with the world and its chakras.

A chakra is an invisible source of energy in your body that guides you on the right path. If you find your chakras, you're all set for life.

While we spoke, I drank a glass of wine. I'm not used to wine: my mom's allergic to alcohol, and Dad only drinks when his chess friend Harry comes to visit. But everyone else was drinking and I didn't want to look like a child.

At first it tasted kind of horrible. But I have to admit, wine can grow on you. Maybe it also depends on the kind of wine. My second glass of wine tasted much better than the first, and the third was best of all. They all came from different bottles, and were even different colours, so that might explain it.

As I sipped the wine, Nigel Sivananda told me that once you were enlightened, you could read a person's aura and even move it around. "Lie down and shut your eyes, Pauline, and I'll show you what I mean," he suggested generously.

It was too crowded to lie down in the living room, so we went to my tiny bedroom — usually a storage room and office, but there's a bed between the filing cabinets and the computer desk. I lay on the bed and shut my eyes.

Nigel Sivananda moved my energy currents and aura without even touching me! I don't know exactly how he did it, but I felt all dizzy and as if I was floating on air. After moving my chakras around, Nigel Sivananda told me to concentrate on the divine spirit in the room. He said everything was divine, from the smallest blade of grass to the great Divine Force of the Universe.

When my chakras were finished moving around, I sat up and Nigel Sivananda gave me an enlightened shoulder massage, using the ancient method of acupressure. While he gave me the massage, he told me about Siddhartha, the great teacher and inventor of the spiritual way to tantric happiness, who became one with the universe.

Suddenly, while Nigel Sivananda was massaging my shoulders, I too became one with the universe! I saw a great light, and all my troubles vanished as if they had never existed. I was speeding away on a cloud to the ends of the tantric universe.

"I see a light!" I blurted out. "I am one with the tantric universe!"

"Brilliant," Nigel said in a serene voice. "You must be an unusually spiritual person, Pauline. You're very lucky, to be so open to the divine spirit."

Then he taught me a brilliant chant, so we could chant together. The chant goes "wa-heh-guru, wa-heh-guru." It opens you to the spiritual oneness of the universe and releases you from desire.

Unfortunately, just at that moment, Siobhan walked into the room and began banging noisily around, opening and closing the filing cabinets. Siobhan is a pretty university student with a ponytail.

As a result of all the clattering, we couldn't chant together. Nigel Sivananda had to go apply his tantric wisdom to Siobhan, because she seemed to be in a very bad mood. I left him to his job and returned with wobbly legs to the living room. There I sat in a daze of enlightenment.

I have now taken the first step in the journey towards Nirvana, the highest stage of understanding and peace. Reaching Nirvana will, from here on, be the goal of my limited, earthly life. Nigel Sivananda has offered to guide me through the process during the two weeks of my visit, and to take me to the ashram with him. The ashram is where all the enlightened people gather.

"We are reviving Indian Buddhism," he explained. "Our ashram combines the ancient teachings of Hinduism with those of Buddhism, gleaning from the wisdom of both." *Gleaning!* Nigel is naturally poetic.

I'm quite "shattered" (that means tired) so I will tell you tomorrow morning about the great city of London.

where Nigel moved my chakras

computer and guestroom

livingroom with boxes about Problems of the World

my grandmother's bedroom

little stove for "heat"

more boxes

very old bathroom

shower with broken faucets

kitchen with shelves

hallway without walls (more like a long balcony)

My grandmother's council flat in London

6

It is the morning of my third day in London. Time is passing quickly! "Time, the devourer of everything." (Ovid. He wrote in Latin.)

Daphne's computer has been fixed, so now I'll be able to make faster progress on this novel. Writing by hand takes a very long time. How did writers manage in the old days? Shakespeare must have been at it from morning to night, considering how much he wrote. Plus he had to dip his pen (or was it a feather?) in ink every few seconds! And you can't correct as easily when you write by hand. It gets messy. There's also no spell-check. I'm glad I'm not a writer in ancient times.

To continue my story: yesterday morning, at breakfast, Daphne gave me a list of places in London that she could take me to, and she told me to mark off the ones I was most interested in seeing, in order of preference. She said, "I don't know your new grown-up personality, dear, so you will have to let me know what you'd like to do."

"I'm not the same person I was before I met Nigel Sivananda," I disclosed, while eating a delicious break-fast of homemade porridge with apricot jam. If you've never tried homemade porridge with apricot jam, I highly recommend it. "I am now on the tantric path towards inner peace and enlightenment," I explained.

"That's wonderful!" Daphne said enthusiastically.

"I still want to go places, though," I quickly added.

"Of course, dear. Enlightenment can take many forms."

Just in case you are like me and live in a small, bor-ing town, and you want to feel sick about how small and boring your life is, here is Daphne's list:

1. The National Gallery. Has paintings by all the Old Masters. This can be combined with a look at Trafalgar Square, full of tourists and pigeons but famous, and a glance at the Royal Horseguards in Whitehall and at No. 10 Downing Street, where the current Prime Minister lives. Nearby is Westminster Abbey — a huge, ancient church where the royals hold their coronations, weddings and funerals at the taxpayers' expense — and Big Ben (the world-famous clock).

2. A walk through Soho to the British Museum, full of historical treasures. We could have supper over in Covent Garden, a lovely area of theatres

and the big Opera House, with open-air entertainment. I think you'd quite enjoy that, Pauline.

3. Tower of London, super touristy but a good reminder of oppression of the weak by the strong.

4. Reconstructed Globe Theatre (where Shakespeare acted). Next door is the Tate Modern art gallery just by the Millennium Bridge, and we can have a beautiful riverside walk!

5. Giant Ferris wheel known as the "London Eye," for a view of London from the air.

6. Capitalist decadence can be observed at Harrods, along with the famous bronze statue of the late Princess Di and her boyfriend Dodi gazing happily at each other, commissioned by Dodi's father.

7. Camden Market. Lots of T-shirts and tattoos, and punks and Goths on display. Perfect for the teenaged tourist.

8. We can take a boat trip on the Thames River to the enormous botanical Kew Gardens, see hundreds of endangered plants and get lost in the Maze. It's a fascinating place, laden with history.

9. Theatre. I'll check what's on.

Well, obviously it was impossible to choose! There's just too much to pack into my short stay. So we decided to go down the list in order, and do a little of everything. That reminded me to ask Daphne whether she had ever heard of *Wake* by Finnegan.

"Finnegan's *Wake*? Oh, it's very famous, dear."

"Do you happen to have a copy?" I asked.

"Siobhan is sure to have one, I'll ask her straight away." "Straight away" means right away.

We took a double-decker bus to the National Gallery. It was brilliant sitting on the top level, in the front seats, looking out. I could gaze at the London streets and the millions of people walking along them. The Christmas decorations added an air of celebration, festivity, merrymaking and bacchanalia.

The British are an interesting people indeed. They may sit quietly and politely in their bus seats, but they draw a lot of attention to themselves nonetheless. Some of them look like characters in an intriguing play. In Canada, we all look pretty much the same, I have to admit. Over here, people are much more original.

Their conversations are different, too. Here is one I heard from the seat behind me, between a white-haired woman and a man who was her son:

Woman: Well, you never do know about rabbits, do you, dear?

Son: Catherine's really quite keen, I must say.

Woman: Yes, well then, I suppose that does come into it.

Son: Of course, Mother, I'm of two minds myself.

Woman: You never do know about rabbits.

Son: Rather sweet, however. ("Rather" is another word you hear quite a lot here.)

Woman: Some might say so.

From this conversation I figured out that the son wanted to get a pet rabbit, either for his wife or more likely for his daughter, and his mother thought it was a completely idiotic thing to do and that only a wimp would get a rabbit just because his daughter (or wife) asked for one. They never came out and said those things, but they understood each other, and even I understood what they meant. I am forced to conclude that people here are rather more polite to their parents than people are in Canada. It was a fascinating study of human nature.

Unfortunately, the woman and her son got off the bus soon after and were replaced by two people who were both on their cell phones but speaking different languages. I couldn't tell whether they knew each other, or what languages they were speaking, but their animated conversations made it hard for me to hear any further exchanges.

I wasn't bored, however. The view from the bus window was truly thrilling. London is filled with buildings that stir the imagination to soaring heights and fill the mind with ideas. You can really see where all those English writers got their inspiration, and what made them write lines like, "He hath awakened from the dream of life" (P. B. Shelley). If I lived here, I would write that way, too.

Daphne has a different view of things. She commented on: the garbage lying in the streets, the homeless people, the drug-dealers, the commercialism, the corporate takeovers, the McDonald's and Starbucks springing up everywhere, the death of culture, the disregard of human needs, exploitation.

I didn't mind her complaints. She has a good sense of humour. When she talks about these things she doesn't sound angry. It's more like she's shaking her head and laughing at how crazy the world is. I can see that acceptance comes with age.

Finally we got to the National Gallery, a vast and majestic edifice, and we began walking through the rooms.

I was speechless indeed. It is hard to believe just

how many talented people there have been throughout the ages. I was sorry Dad wasn't with us. He's an artist, and he'd enjoy seeing all that art. On the other hand, maybe it would depress him to see what he's up against. He's fairly talented, and lately his paintings have been selling rather well, but he has made some very poor choices indeed regarding content. He paints shoes on roads. If he came here, maybe he'd get some ideas for more appropriate topics, like lily ponds or people having a picnic.

Unfortunately, there is only so much art a person can take in. Daphne could have gone on forever. She was very enthusiastic indeed. She kept explaining things to me, and pointing out what this artist did and what that artist did. "Isn't this marvellous! Oh, look, Pauline! See how this eighteenth-century family have been painted in their best clothes, standing in the grounds of their estate, with their grand residence shown in the far distance? That's to demonstrate their wealth and status in society ..."

She glanced at me and noticed that I was getting a little overwhelmed. "Need a break, luvvie?" she asked kindly.

"I think my chakras are fading," I explained.

"Poor you, you must be feeling jet-lagged. How about a spot of lunch?"

So we had a fabulously delicious lunch at Gabby's, a small veggie restaurant in Charing Cross Road, with a counter and lots of little red tables. It was very crowded, and we had to wait for a table. London has quite a prodigious population.

After that we walked up to Tottenham Court Road to catch the No. 73 bus back home, and Daphne told me funny stories about when she first came to London. I still don't know the secret story of why she stayed in England. She was supposed to come over for two weeks to write a story about hot-air balloons for a magazine, but something happened and she ended up staying twenty years. I hope she tells me the secret before I leave.

When we got back to the flat, there was a message for me from Nigel Sivananda! He invited me to see the ashram on Christmas Day. He will come to "collect" me at 6 a.m. so we can get an early start.

I can't wait. In the meantime, I'm practising our chant. *Wa-heh-guru!*

7

Today we went to the British Museum, which was filled with huge statues of gods and Pharaohs and mummies, and many other fascinating remnants from the far and mysterious past.

Daphne told me that you can spend the night in the Egyptian rooms for a fee. That would be cool. Cool, but maybe also a tiny bit terrifying. What if there's some kind of curse? People have been known to die strange deaths after going into Egyptian tombs.

To get to the Museum, we travelled on the No. 73 bus again, and got off in Oxford Street so we could walk back through Soho. There I was treated to a taste of real life. When you live in a small town, real life can pass you right by. In fact, when you live in a small town with only one mall, you may not even know that real life exists.

"The name Soho," Daphne explained, "comes from the sound made by cruel hunters calling their dogs to chase, torment and kill a poor helpless animal for the fun of it." Once, a long time ago, Soho was a park for hunters.

Now Soho is a place where gay culture rules. Imagine if one of those hunters was transported forward in time to the exact same spot today, and found himself in the middle of a gay club! He would be very surprised indeed.

I finally met Daphne's friend Pedro. He had lunch with us at an Indian restaurant on Dean Street. It was packed, and we had to stand in a line (or "queue") to get in, but it was worth the wait. The food was scrumptious. Steaming dishes are placed at the centre of the table, and you help yourself to whatever you want. It's an excellent system. I had several helpings of everything, and by the end of the meal I must say I was ready to burst.

Pedro is a man with a lot of very curly black hair. He's a bit older than Dad, but not as old as Daphne. He looks like he's about to laugh all the time. He was probably quite handsome in his younger days.

Finally, I will get a chance to insert a long passage of dialogue into this novel. One of Zane's Basic Writing Techniques is to include lots of dialogue. I forgot about that, a little. Sorry!

"Did Daphne tell you how we met?" Pedro asked, smiling in a charming way.

"I haven't told Pauline," my grandmother smiled back. "Unless Barbara told her. Did your mother tell you about Pedro?" she queried.

"No," I replied. "Does this have anything to do with the secret reason you stayed in England?"

Daphne and Pedro looked at each other and nodded happily. "I met Pedro on the plane coming into Heathrow," Daphne explained. "He told me that he was escaping a murder charge," she added pleasantly.

"Your grandmother saved my life," Pedro nodded thoughtfully. He seemed to be as impressed now, twenty years later, as he must have been then. "They would never have let me into England. They would have sent me right back to my country, where the executioner was waiting for me."

"It was a political conspiracy," Daphne reassured me.

"They would only let people into England if they had enough money on them, and could show that they were planning to go back home in a few weeks. Daphne gave me all her money, and she told the people at customs that I was her assistant researcher," Pedro beamed.

"I was a journalist back then, as you know," Daphne told me. "I had a visa and a letter from the magazine I was working for, so I was fine. I told the people at customs that Pedro was an expert in the field of aerodynamics. My article was about hot-air balloons."

"I know about the hot-air balloons," I said. "Mom told me that part." What my mom said was, *Your grandmother went off to write about hot-air balloons and ended up with hot air.* I don't know exactly what Mom meant, but I thought it was best not to quote her.

"Your grandmother hid me for nine years, until a new government came to power in my country and I got amnesty. She's a saint," Pedro asserted. (In case you don't know, amnesty is when a government tells convicted people that they're not guilty any more. My grandmother has a whole box just on amnesty.)

"It was the least I could do," Daphne remarked proudly.

"Oh," I said. What else can you say when you find out your grandmother harboured a murderer for nine years?

"If not for her, I would have been tortured and shot," Pedro chuckled.

"What were you planning to do if you hadn't met my grandmother?" I blurted out. Right away I regretted asking something so insensitive, but it was too late.

But Pedro and Daphne just laughed.

"When you're escaping death, you don't have time to worry about anything else," Daphne replied.

"It was love at first sight for both of us," Pedro asserted.

I wondered whether they were still in love, and if so, why they weren't married. Maybe Daphne is too old for Pedro now. I saw a *Dr. Phil* show on that topic.

"How come I don't remember you from when I was five?" I asked.

"You did meet me once or twice," Pedro replied. "You were only a little kid. You probably forgot."

"Maybe because I was developmentally challenged," I said a bit sarcastically. I couldn't help it. I'm still a little bitter about that episode in my life. I think I told you that my parents decided to go on a trip around the world when I was five, and they took me with them but then dumped me in London with Daphne because I was too much trouble. Daphne was very nice to me, but she sent me to a nursery school for kids with developmental problems because it was in a church basement conveniently situated across the street from where she lived. I don't mind that my grandmother sent me to that daycare: I had fun there. What I do mind is that she didn't bother telling the church ladies that I was an ordinary kid and there was nothing wrong with me.

After the meal Pedro left us because he had to rehearse again for *The End of the World in Uncle Sham's*

Basement. Opening night is in four days. Pedro is setting aside two tickets for us.

Daphne and I continued walking along Dean Street, and she showed me where Karl Marx once lived. On my last birthday, Daphne sent me a T-shirt with a picture of a man with a big beard. Now I know who that man is. It's Karl Marx. Daphne assumed I knew all about him, and I was afraid to say I'd never heard of him. I didn't want to upset her. Sometimes it's better to let things pass.

There's a huge, two-storey restaurant in that building now. It's called Quo Vadis. That means "Where are you going?" and the answer is, obviously, "To eat at this restaurant." Very clever.

"The original owner of the restaurant was called Peppino, just like your father." Daphne said. Peppino is a common Italian name, but not everyone understands that. This is a subject I do not like to discuss.

"Marx lived up there," Daphne pointed to the part of the building above the restaurant. "With his wife, their five children and a maid, in only two rooms. Three of his children died right in that house. The water nearby was contaminated, and six hundred people died in just ten days. It was a poor area then."

"I guess they couldn't afford to eat here," I replied, peeking into the restaurant. It looked very expensive.

"William Blake lived in Soho, too," Daphne said. "On the corner of Broad and Marshall Streets."

"I know him!" I said. "We did his poem about the sick rose in school!"

"It's not the same house any more, though. There's a ceramics studio there now, and the street is called Broadwick. We can pass by if you like."

"Sure," I said. It doesn't really matter where you go in Soho; wherever you are, there are cool people all around you. As we walked down the street, I began to feel quite cool myself. And Daphne fit right in. She's extremely cool, I realized. And a lot of people know her. The waiter at the Indian restaurant knew her, the man at the organic bakery knew her, and we passed two women who knew her and stopped to chat. "Chat" is also a word that's used a lot here.

It's funny, but no matter how many things you see on TV or in movies, it's always completely different when you are actually there. You can't become cool by watching cool people on TV. But you can definitely become cool by being in a cool place in person.

Apart from the cool people, there were also quite a few unusual, bizarre and, to be blunt, peculiar people on the street. One man was walking with his little terrier dog on his head, like it was a hat. Another man, who was wearing a bikini bathing-suit bottom and a leather sort of halter top (he must have been freezing), had several balloons strapped to his halter. We also passed an old woman dressed in a fishnet bodysuit, with a purple punk hairdo and a pirate's eye patch. It was possible to see far more of her body than anyone would really want to see. But maybe I'm jumping to conclusions. Maybe these people were on their way to a costume party.

That was my day of contrasts: colourful, modern Soho, followed by Ancient Egypt in the big, airy British Museum in Bloomsbury — from bustling life to the spooky stillness of dead mummies.

The day after tomorrow Nigel Sivananda is coming to take me to the ashram. During the day, he was never far from my thoughts, despite the many stimulating experiences I had in Soho and Bloomsbury. They have made me a wiser and more sophisticated person. But it is tantric enlightenment that will lead the way to true inner peace.

8

"I've endured very, very bitter misery" (Emily Brontë). And I'm never, ever speaking to my mother again.

Yes, my mother. I forgot to mention that Mom was in Greece with Agatone, her new boyfriend, and they were planning to meet us in London on the way back to Canada. At the time, I thought it was an okay plan. It never occurred to me that my mom would completely destroy my vacation, my happiness and my life.

At first, everything was going better than I could have imagined in my wildest dreams. On December 24th, I mostly slept during the day. I think the jet lag finally caught up with me. Then in the evening we volunteered at a homeless shelter, handing out meals to the destitute. Daphne's Jewish like Mom, and I'm half-Jewish, so we didn't mind celebrating Christmas in depressing surroundings. I'd tell you more about it but I'm too impatient to relate the events at the ashram, so I'll get back to the homeless later. Sorry, Zane!

The following morning, Nigel Sivananda picked me up (or as they say here, "collected me" — which sounds as if I am made of a lot of tiny pieces lol) early in the morning.

As soon as I saw his blue eyes piercing into me, my heart began to pound. He is the handsomest person I have ever seen in real life. To see him is to melt. I mean, my boyfriend Yoshi is cute, very cute indeed. But it's different when someone's a guru. I couldn't believe Nigel Sivananda had come just for me — ordinary Pauline. When I climbed into the passenger seat of his car, I felt I was going for a ride with a movie star. I was almost trembling with excitement. However, my goal is peace and serenity, so I did my best to control my worldly emotions.

The ashram is quite far from Stoke Newington, or "Stokie" — the part of North London where Daphne lives. It took over an hour to get there. London is a large city.

"Normally it would take longer," Nigel said, "but there isn't much traffic because of the holiday. When you're stuck in traffic, you must make yourself one with it. It's not your adversary, but part of yourself. We are trapped inside our egos. The minute we free our-selves from our egos, we will never again be annoyed by something like a traffic jam."

Just then a driver cut in front of him out of nowhere. Nigel was very serene, even though we nearly had an accident. "Mercy," he said, as he slammed on the brakes. He has put his wisdom to good use.

The ashram is in a beautiful old house with polished wood. It has almost no furniture and it's very quiet. All the people are at peace, so they don't need to talk a lot or make a lot of noise. They are lost deep inside their enlightened spirits.

We had breakfast around a long, rectangular wooden table. We sat on the floor instead of on chairs — luckily the table had short legs. There were twelve Buddhists at breakfast. Most of them were Nigel's age, but two were much older. The older Buddhists were bald and wore long brownish-grey robes. Maybe they're the teachers. The other Buddhists were dressed mostly in sweat pants and white T-shirts. It's a casual ashram.

The meal was somewhat unusual. In the centre of the table there were a few plates of some kind of spicy flat tortilla, and two large bowls filled with a hot cooked dish called bulgur, which is like rice but crunchier. There were also two jugs of fruit juice and a few bananas. Not a wide variety, I admit, but all of it was quite tasty. I had two bananas, five tortillas and two helpings of the bulgur. Then I noticed that no one else had seconds. They are more advanced on the road to freeing themselves from desire.

I couldn't help noticing how pretty one of the girls was. She was dressed all in white: a white dress, white leggings and a cute white scarf tied around her head. Only her slippers weren't white. They were flip-flops with little Mickey Mouse designs on the straps.

Her big eyes and shiny skin reminded me of one of the paintings at the National Gallery — the one where a woman is fleeing from a dragon. When she saw that I was looking at her, she gave me a warm smile.

Sitting on the floor to eat was very cool. I also noticed that no one talked. We ate in deep silence. You need silence to concentrate on your chakras.

After breakfast, Nigel showed me around. There wasn't much to see. There are four meditation rooms on the main floor of the ashram, as well as a really tidy office. Buddhism is like Christianity that way. Churches are also extremely tidy, in my experience.

The meditation rooms were mostly bare, apart from some statues and candles. A third bald man who hadn't come to breakfast (he has truly conquered desire!) was meditating in one of the rooms, so we tip-toed away. We didn't want to disturb him in his spiritual quest.

The bedrooms are upstairs. Some people share,

and some have their own rooms, depending on how spiritual they are and also on how much rent they pay. Nigel has his own room, right at the top of the stairs. It's tiny, though. I think it was once a closet.

If I describe the rest of the day, you might think it was boring, but I wasn't bored for a single minute. I learned all kinds of new chants, which Nigel and I practised in his room for a few hours. Then he gave me another ancient massage, after which he had to go out to work for a few hours. He gave me two books about the great Siddhartha to read while he was gone. I also had a conversation with the pretty girl. Her name is Eloise. She's very friendly. She told me she's from Peru, originally.

"Then I lived in Holland with my mother, then in Switzerland with my father, and now I've ended up here," she said casually. Some people have such exotic lives!

We chatted about the great teacher Siddhartha, about the road to enlightenment, and about how I met Nigel. Eloise was curious to hear what I thought of him. "He's very spiritual," I told her. Eloise agreed.

Just before suppertime, Nigel returned and the two of us went out for a walk in the park. It was chilly out, so he put his arm around my shoulder to warm me up. I almost fainted.

After that we had supper at the long table again. This time there was a CD playing of a guru giving advice during the whole meal. His words were full of wisdom. Anyone following his advice can reach Nirvana in no time.

There was more chanting and meditation after supper. Then we all retired to our rooms and Nigel told me about himself. To earn a living, he poses for books that tell you the story with photographs and little balloons coming out of people's mouths. I also found out that Nigel has a degree from Oxford University, but he's not interested in living a superficial life. Even if he wanted to live a superficial life, there aren't any jobs in Comparative Philology, which is what he studied. In case you're wondering, Comparative Philology means comparing foreign languages.

After a while we both noticed that it was getting late. "Would you like to sleep over?" he asked. "We can practise redirecting our tantric energy by refraining from physical contact whilst sharing the same bed."

How could I say no?

"I just need to ask Daphne," I said.

"Oh, there's no need. I already told her you might be back tomorrow. We go to sleep rather early, though, as we're up in the wee small hours of the morning for our morning meditation."

Canadians never say poetic things like "wee small hours of the morning" or "whilst."

"That's all right," I said. "I'm rather shattered from all the chanting." I didn't want to appear enslaved to the physical world, so I didn't add that my back was also killing me. It's not easy to sit in the lotus position for hours on end. Buddhists don't believe in chairs.

Nigel's bed is a thin futon mattress on a wooden platform. Not too comfy, but I didn't mind! I was so excited I could hardly breathe.

Eloise lent me pyjamas (white, of course), and Nigel Sivananda and I lay down side by side.

After about ten minutes, Nigel said in a rather hoarse voice, "By the way, how old are you exactly, Pauline?" Then he coughed to clear his throat.

"Fourteen," I said. "But I'll be fifteen in nine days."

"Fourteen! You're joking!" Nigel momentarily lost his serenity.

I was quite hurt at first. I thought he meant that I looked younger than my age.

"What did you think?" I asked with a trembling voice.

"I thought you were considerably older." He didn't sound at all friendly. Then he got up, opened the door to his room all the way, got back in bed, turned his back to me and began to snore loudly.

I admit I was a little disappointed. I was hoping for at least a goodnight hug before we redirected our tantric energy. But I was exhausted, so I fell asleep almost immediately.

Since I want to remember this day by itself, without what happened next, I will end the chapter here, and tell you about the nightmare that followed in the next chapter.

9

At first I thought I was having a bad dream in which my mom was banging on the door of the ashram and shouting, "Let me in! Let me in this minute!"

Then I realized that it wasn't a dream. Someone was banging on the door and shouting in a very loud voice. The voice sounded a lot like my mom's. She used to be an opera singer, and believe me, she can project if she wants to.

I froze. I was hoping that if I didn't move, the voice would go away, as well as the banging. However, someone else must have opened the door, because the voice was suddenly much closer, and it definitely belonged to my mom. "Where is she? Where's my daughter?" she shouted at the top of her lungs.

By some kind of mother-radar she stormed right into Nigel's room. Or maybe she chose it because it was right near the stairs and the door was open.

"What is going on here, may I ask?!" she blared.

"Mom, calm down," I said, my voice quivering

with shame and a strong desire to die on the spot. "You're upsetting everyone's serenity."

My mom stared at me. I knew that look. She was trying to decide whether to feel sorry for me or blame me. Thank goodness, Agatone's head appeared suddenly behind her. Agatone is a much more balanced person than my mom. By now Nigel was standing by the bed, trying to smile and be polite, but looking quite worried and not at all at one with the universe.

"How do you do?" he said. He is so wonderful!

The other Buddhists also tried to mutter a few reassuring things. Eloise offered my mom tea. One of the bald men bowed to her. My mom ignored them both.

To make a long, agonizing story short, I quickly got dressed, and without looking at anyone or saying a word, I ran out of the ashram.

There was a taxi parked outside. The meter was already at forty-five pounds, which is almost a hundred dollars.

Humiliating me in front of Nigel and the entire ashram was not enough for my mom. She felt that the evening would not be complete unless she humiliated me in front of the taxi driver, too.

Agatone tried to calm her down, but he didn't have much success. My mom was in a lunatic state. I doubt very much that he's going to want to continue dating her after this. The only sane adult in my life, and I will never see him again.

He said in a jovial, reassuring voice, "You see, everything is fine, Barbara. Pauline is safe and sound."

My mother acted as if she didn't even hear him. "This is so typical! So absolutely typical!" she vociferated. "Completely irresponsible and unreliable. My mother is living in a fantasy world of her own, where everyone is good. You could sell her the Brooklyn Bridge without even trying. You could sell her the Arizona Desert!"

My grandmother does *not* think everyone is good, obviously. On the contrary, she spends all her time talking about how the world is full of people who are cruel and immoral. But when Mom is in one of her moods, it's best not to contradict her.

"Look at that Pedro business. Don't even get me started on Pedro. He totally used her for nine years, and has he ever paid her back a single penny? What did she get out of it? She gave up everything for him."

My mother obviously does not understand true love.

"If you knew, if you only knew," Mom went on. "This is what my whole life has been like! I can't trust her for even one minute."

Since my mom seemed to be angrier with Daphne than with me, I risked saying something. "You trusted her when I was five," I pointed out.

"Yes, and what did she do? Sent you to a school for disturbed children. Took you to demonstrations against nuclear facilities. Exposed you to tear gas!"

"The children weren't disturbed," I mumbled. "I liked it there." I never thought I'd be defending Daphne for sending me to that daycare.

"And now, letting you go off with a total stranger, who could be a psychotic child killer for all she knows, to spend the night at some cult hippie ashram."

"Grandma knows the guy who took me. He's her friend."

"We can discuss all of this in the morning," Agatone tried once again to change the topic. "Over a nice breakfast."

He obviously doesn't know my mom if he thought he could stop her so easily. She went right on, like a bull heading for a red cape. "That's not what she told us. She told us she didn't know this man from Adam. He's someone's friend. A girl with an Irish name."

"Siobhan?"

"Yes, that's right. Siobhan. And she lets you go off with this total stranger to some cult where, for all she knows, they have orgies and do drugs. And she says it's okay for you to sleep over!"

"They're Buddhists, Mom. Buddhists are very peaceful people."

"So what exactly were you doing in this person's bed? Now I have to worry about AIDS and pregnancy not just at my job, but with my own daughter. Thanks to your grandmother."

All this in front of the taxi driver!

"Nothing happened, Mom," I whispered, hoping she'd take the cue from me. "We were redirecting our tantric energy."

Unfortunately, my mom has never whispered in her life.

"I don't even believe my ears!" she shouted. "What are you, six?"

This was too much. I folded my arms, turned my face to the window and made myself completely deaf.

It worked. My mother immediately shifted from Angry Mode to Guilty Mode. She can do that in one second flat.

"Oh, I'm sorry, sweetheart," she said. "I was just so worried."

"Very understandable," Agatone said, sounding relieved.

"He did look like a nice boy," Mom had to admit.

(Nigel is *not* a boy, but I let it pass.) "But how could Daphne take such a chance?"

"I think she said she knows that group," Agatone commented.

"Buddhism is about renouncing desire," I explained patiently.

"Desire is much easier to renounce in separate beds," my mom stated. "I'm sorry I got so angry at you, darling. It's Daphne I'm angry at."

I know that Mom has many complaints about my grandmother. She's been making small, bitter comments on that subject as far back as I can remember.

Suddenly I thought of Nigel standing near the bed and saying, "How do you do?" in an unhappy voice. I burst into tears. He would never speak to me again! My mother had ruined my enlightenment forever.

She kept apologizing, but I refused to forgive her. That put her in a bad mood all over again.

10

When we got back to Daphne's flat I marched straight to my little bedroom and shut the door. I was still crying. "My eyes like some fountain with tears overflow" (Ballad by Anonymous Woman).

Unfortunately, Daphne's apartment has thin walls, and I could hear every word that was being spoken in the living room. It was half-fascinating, half-sickening.

My mother was talking to my grandmother. Actually, she was more ranting than talking. Mom had a long, long list of all the things my grandmother did that she's still angry about. Some of them had to do with my Aunt Hilda, Mom's sister. I only met Hilda once, when I was small. She lives in Vancouver, and she and Mom haven't been on speaking terms ever since Hilda's wedding, when they had a fight over the bow on the bridesmaid's dress.

Here is a summary of some of Mom's accusations:

1. "Dad left that money for us. For Hilda and me. He paid into that insurance policy for

years. And what did you do? What did you do, Mummy? You gave it all away. Every single penny. Bit by bit, until it was all gone to all the good causes in the universe. And what was left for me? For your own daughter who was about to start university? Nothing. Not one penny. I could have been settled for life. I wouldn't have had to worry about bills and rent and food and Pauline. But no. You had to give it to every bleeding-heart cause in the world."

2. "Never once, not one time even, did you encourage me in my singing. Maybe I would have stuck to opera, if I'd had some support. You were even too busy to come to my concerts. Off on some demonstration."

3. "The wretched of the earth were always more important than me. You never really cared about me."

4. "I couldn't count on you for anything. You promised you'd be somewhere at six o'clock, and you never got there. There was always something more important. Remember that time I waited in the snowstorm after the party? I almost got frostbite because of your irresponsibility!"

5. "You ruined my shower cap." (I may not have heard right.)

6. "You liked Hilda a million times better than me. What about those goldfish? That totally proves it. You didn't care at all about my feelings when she poured that orange juice in the tank. All you cared about was the fish. The fish were more important to you than your own daughter."

7. "You read that stupid poem at Dad's funeral without even asking me. You asked Hilda, and that was enough for you. My opinion didn't count at all. What does Hilda know about poetry? She's an accountant! That poem was an insult to Dad's memory. He hated the Grateful Dead."

I think at this point I drifted off. I dreamed I was on a raft in the middle of the ocean and Nigel was trying to throw me a rope to hold on to, but the rope kept slipping out of my hand.

Now it's morning and I'm typing on the computer in my bedroom. It's quiet in the apartment, so I guess everyone is still asleep. Mom probably kept Daphne up all night with her list.

Nigel, Nigel, Nigel Sivananda! I need you to advise

me about ridding myself of these worldly feelings of pain and misery. Yet how can I ever face you again? My chakras have been crushed, pulverized, smitten and torn asunder.

11

My mother has left London. She and Agatone took an early flight back to Canada. That information was welcome, under the circumstances.

She left me a note:

Dear sweetheart,

We decided to take an early flight back, as I have a lot to do at home. Have a fabulous time for the remainder of your trip. I'm sorry we're missing your birthday — we left a present for you with Daphne. She has promised to keep an eye on you. You may go to the ashram during the day only. Do not have sex, please, tantric or otherwise. You are too young. I hope it is not too late to say this.

Love, hugs, and sorry I upset you. I was worried.

Mom

How can she be so inappropriate? Is this a normal note for a mother to write to her young, innocent daughter?

Maybe the problem is that she works with women who have just come out of jail, helping them settle in a new life. Those women can be quite impulsive.

Well, it's fine with me that she's gone. Daphne and I are managing perfectly well on our own. My mother's clothes would only be an embarrassment in a place like Soho, not to mention her overly loud, window-rattling, ear-piercing voice. If she'd rather go back to Ghent, Ontario, than spend a few days taking in the wonders of London with her mother and her only daughter, I have no objections. I only feel bad for Agatone. He would have had a good time.

Daphne tried to be her usual optimistic self today, but I could tell my mom's visit had taken its toll. We both needed to do something peaceful, so we skipped down our list, all the way to number 8: Thames River (pronounced "TEMS" for some reason) and Kew Gardens.

"A visit to Kew is just what the doctor ordered," Daphne said, trying to sound lighthearted. But the pouches under her eyes looked more pouchy than usual. She has aged overnight.

We left right after breakfast. Even though it's December, it isn't all that cold out, just sort of damp. In Canada we'd already be trudging through snow.

Daphne was quiet at first. On the boat trip down

to Kew she didn't say a single word, though she sighed several times. She was lost in thought. I, on the other hand, was quite excited to be travelling down the River Thames by boat. Oh, London, London, how I love you!

When we reached the Gardens, Daphne led me straight to a huge greenhouse (only here they call it a "glass house" — much more poetic!) called the Temperate House. But it's not like any greenhouse you've ever been to in Ontario. I mean, it's not like some boring plant store with rows of pots on long tables or on the floor. This was more like stepping into a steamy jungle, overflowing with plant life. There were quite a few tourists, too, but they weren't the noisy kind. Maybe plants make people quiet by example.

I followed Daphne past hanging vines, giant leaves, misty waterfalls and exotic flowers with strange Latin names. If I lived in London I, too, would come here when my soul was weary from unjust accusations.

Finally, as we stood staring at the world's largest indoor plant, which is fifty-two feet high — you have to climb up winding stairs to see the top of it — Daphne said, "I'm sorry about yesterday, Pauline."

"What do you have to apologize for?" I asked. "My mom is the one I'm angry at."

"I should never have exposed you to that situation."

"But you were right about everything. The ashram was a safe place. And it wasn't fair to ask Nigel to drive me all the way home and back twice in one day. He had a very long day of chants and enlightenment and being photographed."

"All the same, dear …"

"I think Mom is being unfair," I said supportively.

"Oh, there's no fair or unfair in families!" Daphne laughed. "Families were invented to make everyone feel hard done by. Isn't this place a paradise? It always cheers me up to be here. And the smells!" She breathed in deeply and shut her eyes.

I must say, I was relieved that Daphne was cheering up. Her statement on families was profound indeed.

After a few seconds, Daphne reopened her eyes and smiled. "There are still some vestiges of intelligence and humanity here and there, amidst the evil," she said.

"Indeed," I concurred.

"I hope you realize, Pauline, that your mother's change of schedule has nothing to do with not wanting to be with you. She would have loved to stay, but I think she was worried about damaging my relationship with you."

"We're better off without her," I said grumpily.

"I certainly am enjoying your visit!" Daphne said tactfully.

"Will I ever see Nigel again, I wonder?" I muttered sadly, as we continued to weave our bodies through the bursting foliage.

"Of course, dear. I already rang him up and he's coming by tonight for tea and a chat."

I had mixed feelings about that news. How can I face Nigel after last night? On the other hand, how can I give up a lifetime of spiritual enlightenment under his guidance? I have just started out, and the road is long. It would be even longer, but luckily the great teacher Siddhartha already ruled out some paths that didn't work.

"This *protea* plant suddenly bloomed after 160 years," Daphne said, reading a sign. "Now 120 types of *proteas* are endangered," she added with a sigh. "Do you want to see the last surviving specimen of one type of tree? It's a lone male."

I never knew trees had males and females. And, frankly, I wish I still didn't know. Many, many things are better left unspoken and in the dark.

Zane warns writers about too much description. *Get on with the story!* he advises. So I won't tell you about the other things we saw at Kew. I'll only say that if you are ever a tourist in London, don't miss it. Even if you are not into plants, you should go, as it is immense and filled with palaces, exhibitions of the way life was long ago, royal dollhouses, breathtaking flowers, fountains, a crazy maze and many more incredible sights. If I lived here I'd be a Kew addict, too, just like Daphne.

Nigel Sivananda is arriving in an hour. I have to shampoo my hair, put on eye shadow and get into a meditative state, so I'd better sign off. Daphne is baking scones. The sublime odour of baking will definitely help my chakras recover their equilibrium.

12

I haven't written all week because I was too busy. I've seen more of London, I went to a brilliant New Year's Eve party, I experienced an extremely heightened level of consciousness, and I saw the best play of my life. I also turned fifteen.

First I'll tell you about the play. It was the one Pedro was in. I didn't think it was going to be very good because my last experience with amateurs was not encouraging (described in my first novel). But it turns out that Pedro is not an amateur. He is a superb actor, along with all the other marvellous actors who were in the play. In case you forgot, the play was called *The End of the World in Uncle Sham's Basement*. It was in a small but pleasant theatre at the end of an alley, through a billiard room, down some stairs, through a corridor and past a massage parlour.

It was the funniest and best play I have ever seen or will ever see again. I laughed from beginning to end. It was about a crazy man who lives in a basement apartment and all his crazy neighbours. There was also a rapper on a skateboard who skated across the stage every now and then. Every time he appeared the audience had hysterics. All he had to do was show up and everyone began to laugh.

Pedro was one of the neighbours. He was called Pedro in the play, too. He was helping Uncle Sham prepare for the end of the world by collecting bar codes from frozen fish-stick boxes. Uncle Sham was convinced that corporations were going to take over the world and only people with bar codes would be allowed to live.

In between helping Uncle Sham collect bar codes, Pedro talked to his cat and to Saint Jude, patron saint of desperate situations. He consulted them both regarding his next step with his girlfriend Manfreda, a manicurist and grave digger.

I'm sure this hilarious play will receive worldwide recognition. It hasn't been reviewed yet.

I don't have much to say about my birthday. I didn't celebrate it because I'm freeing myself from the shackles of ego. What is a birthday after all, if not a fleeting illusion of the prison that is Self? (Mom's birthday present was a necklace from Greece, btw. It's quite pretty, in fact, with tiny blue stones. I'm wearing it as I write.)

As for my heightened level of consciousness, it was a blissful, ecstatic, radiant, rapturous and Elysian experience.

It happened after a long day of chants, meditation and breathing. Nigel decided to take me out to eat at a whole-foods, organic, vegan restaurant.

It was a brilliant place. The waiters were dressed as if they were on their way to a super-cool nightclub and had just stopped to do some serving on the way. They all seemed to be good friends with each other, chatting and laughing together at the counter.

Nigel and I had fennel and parsnip soup, spiced noodles, wild mushroom pie and berry mousse for desert. Every mouthful was divine.

Suddenly, we saw something strange. All the waiters, who were congregated behind the counter, ducked down so they were out of sight, and then quickly crawled into the kitchen on their hands and knees!

"Must be someone from the dole office," Nigel explained, looking at the couple who had just entered the restaurant. I didn't want to display my ignorance, so I didn't ask for further clarification. I have to remember to ask Daphne what "dole" means.

After the meal, we drank ginger tea with organic brown sugar (served by the owner — the waiters were still in hiding). As we sipped our tea in a profound meditative state, Nigel took my hand and held it in his. Then he lifted my hand to his angelic lips and kissed it. That was when it happened. I felt shivers of joyful peace piercing my soul and carrying me to new heights of awareness and understanding. The way of Siddhartha appeared with clarity and light.

"I am approaching Nirvana," I whispered.

Nigel didn't answer. He only smiled serenely.

We left the restaurant and walked hand in hand, enjoying our oneness with the universe. The Christmas lights on the streets glittered like the light in our hearts. And then, under a big poster for Levi's Jeans, Nigel Sivananda kissed me, his lips lightly touching mine. "There is no blissful peace until one passes beyond the agony of life and death" (Siddhartha).

How will I leave England? It is here that I have passed beyond the agony of life and death into blissful peace. How can I bear to be separated from Nigel Sivananda, my guru, my wise teacher?

After we kissed, I said, "I know I'm not supposed to be attached to things of the world, but I will miss you, Nigel."

"Luckily, there's e-mail," he reassured me. "We can stay in touch on a daily basis, sharing our experiences in our pursuit of spiritual growth."

That has been my week. Oh, I almost forgot. I also went on the London Eye. Awesome!

13

I'm writing by hand once again, this time because I'm on the plane going back to Canada. Despite the fact that I'm in an airplane, I feel elated.

> *My heart is like a singing bird,*
> *Whose nest is in a watered shoot.*
> *My heart is like an apple tree,*
> *Whose boughs are bent with thickset fruit.*
> (Christina Rossetti, she knows how to put things.)

I can't wait to tell my boyfriend Yoshi about my new spiritual path. He may not understand about the kiss, though. I think I'll just stick to the search for enlightenment. He's a deep person, I'm sure he'll be very interested. I hope he likes the London Underground mouse pad I got for him.

I have three seats all to myself, so I'm going to stretch out now and meditate. This will help me deal with my worldly attachment to life and my fear of crashing.

See you later (I hope)!

14

To my great surprise, Yoshi came with Dad to pick me up at the airport. How romantic! I'd almost forgotten how cute Yoshi is. It was pleasant to be reminded again. We couldn't hug, unfortunately, as Dad and Bunny were there, too.

Dad said, "Welcome back, Pauline. We've an Extreme Cold warning today. It's minus twenty-nine with the wind chill." Then he handed me a dorky woollen hat and mitts. My parents refuse to understand that no young person with a shred of self-respect wears that type of hat or mitts, no matter how many of these sad items they get from well-meaning relatives on their birthdays.

"No, thanks," I said. "I'll just button up."

"How was your trip, dear?" Bunny gushed. Bunny, in case you forgot, is the old woman my dad is dating. At first I didn't like Bunny, then I decided she was okay. Now I understand that everyone is part of the same karmic energy. "We're having crazy weather," she continued. "One day it's as warm as spring, the next it's suddenly a million below zero. We're destroying this planet with fuel emissions."

I guess old people are obsessed with the state of the planet. You'd think they would be the ones who are least worried, seeing as they're the ones who will die soonest. "How are you? How was London? Tell all."

"I had a brilliant time, indeed," I said. "Thanks for coming to collect me. I'm utterly shattered."

We had to walk forever to find Dad's pick-up in the parking garage. That garage is the size of our entire town.

I have to admit, I was pretty cold. Yoshi noticed, and lent me his black wool scarf. On top of being cute, he has a kind heart.

I wrapped the scarf around my ears, which were slowly going numb. Finally, after about half an hour, we found the truck. I was practically a block of ice by then.

Dad and Bunny got in front, and Yoshi and I sat in the seat behind them. My dad has a pick-up truck so he can transport his paintings and art supplies from place to place. The truck is quite old, and it used to smell of cat pee, due to an unfortunate accident with Stormy Weather, my adorable cat. Dad tried to get rid of the smell without success, until Bunny gave him a special potion that worked wonders. She definitely has her good points.

"I know how dismal airplane food can be," Bunny said, as she handed out homemade cream cheese and olive sandwiches on delicious rye bread. As I said, definite good points.

Yoshi's reaction to my quest for enlightenment was a little disappointing. As we munched on the sandwiches, I told him about chakras and karma and Nigel Sivananda and the ashram and the great teacher Siddhartha. I'm glad I decided not to mention that I reached Nirvana for a few seconds under a Levi's Jeans poster. I also didn't mention sharing a bed with Nigel Sivananda, or the tantric massages. I didn't want him to get the wrong impression.

Yoshi was very quiet. He didn't seem at all enthusiastic.

Finally I said, "Isn't this all fascinating?"

He said in a gloomy voice, "My whole family is technically Buddhist."

I was stunned. I didn't know I had a Buddhist boyfriend, and that there was a Buddhist family right in the middle of my life!

However, upon further questioning, I found that Yoshi and his family have never chanted, meditated or breathed deeply and serenely in their lives. Nor do they sit on the floor. I guess they are lapsed Buddhists.

I gave Yoshi the mouse pad I bought for him. He seemed to like it.

It was strange coming back to Ghent after London. I never noticed how quiet our town is. You can hear a shoe drop.

I invited Yoshi over and offered to show him some of my chants. I was looking forward to resuming our intimacy. Cuddling up with Yoshi whilst discussing the futility of earthly existence would be pleasant indeed. Yoshi seems to have grown handsomer during my time away. I love his black hair and cute eyes, and his tanned skin makes me think of toast and honey.

But he was suddenly in a big rush. He said he had an indoor soccer game to prepare for.

I was sad to see him go. I had so much to tell him, and I wanted to hear what he did while I was away. Probably not much — what is there to do in Ghent? I hope I haven't made him feel bad that he hasn't travelled to distant lands (though he did spend a summer in Japan when he was six).

But people who do sports can be a little fanatic. As I mentioned earlier, my best friend, Genevieve, is a figure skater, and she used to worry if she had to miss even one day of practice. So I tried not to take it personally.

Stormy Weather was really happy to see me. She's more like a dog that way. She kept meowing and rubbing herself against my leg. At least someone is happy I'm back.

"Mom wants you to go over for supper," Dad informed me. "Just give her a call, she'll come pick you up."

When my mom answered the phone she acted as if I'd been lost for days in a wild forest and a rescue team had just found me. "Pauline!" she screeched. "Are you coming over? Agatone's cooked a special meal for you. And we have some very exciting news."

I unpacked while munching on Bunny's carrot cake, which she baked especially for me. It had *Welcome Back* written on it in white icing. My bedroom is right next to the kitchen, which has its advantages. It's easy to access food whilst doing other things. The whole upstairs of our house is Dad's studio, and the bedrooms are on the ground floor, except that now there's only my bedroom. When my parents divorced, Dad moved his bed upstairs to his studio, and the den that used to be Mom and Dad's bedroom is now a room filled with junk.

Mom picked me up just as I was helping myself to another slice of carrot cake. But she didn't tell me the exciting news right away. She waited until I was biting into Agatone's feta and potato pie.

I'm still trying to digest it. (The news, not the pie.)

15

The meal, and the news, took place in my mom's luxury condo apartment, which she can't afford. However, the high rent of the condo will not be a problem for much longer.

I noticed when I entered the condo that Mom was in a very strange mood. She was giggling and being quite childish. Agatone was also laughing for no reason that I could see.

We sat down to eat, and my mom and Agatone kept looking at each other like two-year-olds who have a stupid secret they think is a big deal, like where they hid their chocolate-chip cookies.

Finally Mom said, "Sweetheart, we have some big news. Agatone and I have decided to get married."

That didn't seem like such big news. People get married every day, and Agatone is not at all a bad choice, considering my mom's previous boyfriends, about whom you can read in my first novel. As long as they get married quietly and maturely in a judge's office and I do not have to be present, I have no objection. Also, I'm not calling Agatone "Dad." To me he will always be "Agatone."

"That's nice," I said, noting to myself that Agatone's cooking talents were a definite plus. I'd have good meals permanently. "This pie is great," I added.

"Darling, we've also decided to move to Greece for six months — if you agree, that is."

I stopped eating in mid-bite. "How come?" I asked.

"Well, Agatone has a job he needs to get back to, and I've fallen in love with Greece. I may be able to teach English there, and I need a change of scene. This weather is ridiculous!" she added in a strong voice. Dad had already told me that while I was getting enlightened in London over the past week, back here there was a non-stop series of snowstorms, windstorms and ice storms. Some people were without electricity for two whole days.

"Okay," I said. I mean, they weren't really going to change their plans if I said no, and why should I say no? I'm not going to stand in the way of my mom's plans for love and good weather. If Agatone and sunshine are more important to her than being with her daughter, that is entirely her affair.

"Darling, are you sure? As I said, it would only be

for six months. If you want to come with us, we can look for a tutor, and you can complete the school year there. Or, if you want to stay here, we'll send e-mails every day and we can talk on Instant Messenger, too."

Instant Messenger — is she mad? What is it with parents? How can they be so intensely clued out? Imagine if someone found out that you were talking to *your parent* on Messenger!! I'm getting queasy just thinking about it.

"Don't even think about trying to talk to me on Instant Messenger," I said in a determined, resolute and final voice.

"Whatever you want, honey-pie," she quickly added. She's never called me so many lovey-dovey names in such a short time. Usually it's more spread out.

"I'd rather stay here," I decided. What would I do in Greece? I don't even speak the language. And I don't want a tutor. What if the tutor has bad breath?

"I won't go if you want me to stay," Mom said uncertainly.

"I'll be perfectly fine without you," I assured her. At least no one will nag me continually and endlessly about housework chores, I thought but did not say out loud.

We moved on to other subjects. I didn't have much to say about those subjects. I ate in meditative silence, removed from the hurly-burly of our temporary and fleeting existence.

Mom didn't eat a thing. "Don't you like the food?" I asked her.

"Oh, I'm just not that hungry," Mom mumbled. She looked at Agatone and they both smiled again in that immature way.

Anyhow, Mom is subletting the condo, and she also decided to sell the decaying house we lived in last year. She's selling it to Bright Homes Realty. They plan to tear the house down and build a triplex on the property. At first she rejected their offer, but they've raised it, so everything is working out all perfect. How lucky for her.

As for me, I get to live with Dad full-time, whether Bunny is there or not.

That is all I have to report. I have jet lag, I think, because indeed I must say I'm feeling a wee bit muddled and rather shattered.

I also feel shocked, to tell you the truth, at the news of my mom's six-month desertion of her only child. In the past, I thought she loved me.

16

I haven't written all week because the homework situation was out of hand, untenable, indefensible and cruel.

Each teacher seems to think that we don't have any other classes. So they give us an hour of homework, which to them seems reasonable. What they are forgetting is that we have five other teachers who are also giving us an hour of homework, except for our English teacher, Ms. Plessix, who is giving us seventeen hours of homework per day. Yesterday she ordered us to write 500 sentences using the word "its" correctly, so that we would never get "it's" and "its" mixed up again in our lives. She said if she sees one more incorrect "it's" she will have a nervous breakdown.

In my opinion she is already in the midst of a nervous breakdown.

She pointed out that the error is so widespread that she's seen it in letters from the bank, quotes from reviews on billboards and the back of cereal boxes. She said that soon she will see it in the *New York Times* and at that point she will know that civilization, the little that remains of it, has collapsed.

If the mistake is so widespread, how will our one small class make a difference? We're only thirty-six kids.

I found an easy solution to the assignment, however, thanks to my trustworthy thesaurus, which has come to my rescue once again. I looked up "fish" and I wrote: *The albacore is in its pond. The alewife is in its pond. The amberjack is in its pond.* And so on, all the way down the list. When I ran out of fish, I moved on to birds: *The aberdevine is in its nest. The adjutant bird is in its nest. The albatross is in its nest.*

Poor Harold Hamovitch, he got the "it's" and "its" reversed. He has to do the entire assignment over.

Ms. Plessix has no inner peace.

Speaking of inner peace, I'm rather disappointed in the lack of interest shown by my friends in the ways of enlightenment.

Leila interrupted me in the middle of my description of deep breathing to say, "Hey, before I forget, Pauline, there's a school dance in two weeks. It's going to be lame, but better than nothing. Did you hear what happened with Augusta and Ryan? Her parents made him break up with her. They called his parents and told them off, just like in *Romeo and Juliet*, except that Ryan didn't try to see Augusta after that. Her parents said she was too young to be going out with someone like Ryan. So now she's dating Joel, only it's a secret, her parents don't know this time — because he's even older than Ryan. By four months. I can't decide who to go to the dance with, Dave and Don, who do you think I should choose? I mean, how can you choose between identical twins? They're identical!"

I was interested in Leila's news, especially the part about Ryan, a cute guy from New York who deceived me in September into thinking we were going out, as a result of which I broke up with Yoshi, only to discover that Ryan wasn't interested in me after all and was going out with Augusta instead. This was not exactly surprising, as Augusta is sophisticated, pretty and speaks four-and-a-half languages. Her parents are millionaires, they take her all over the world, she gets to meet famous people, and last week her mother was interviewed by *Vanity Fair* for an article on Equestrian Women. They took a photo of Augusta and her mother next to one of their horses.

So you can see how Augusta is a better match for Ryan, who's in grade ten, went to an alternative school in New York and is best friends with the son of a music manager who manages the same famous people Augusta meets at hotels in California. Augusta also has more confidence than me. She feels that to know her is to love her, while I feel that to know me is to like me or not like me, depending on whether we have anything in common. Anyhow it was lucky — very lucky indeed — that Yoshi took me back after I dropped him for Ryan.

Even though I was interested in Leila's update, I confess I was hoping for a little more enthusiasm about my new levels of consciousness. However, Leila is not interested in matters of the spirit. She's becoming more like her mother, whose life revolves around whether people are flossing or not. (She's a dentist.)

Rachel was even less interested. She said, "Don't talk to me about religion. I hate it all." She has recently rebelled against her strange religious upbringing, which doesn't allow television, radios or even toasters. She'd be in big trouble, but she has only her old, frail grandmother to rebel against, and her grandmother doesn't have the energy to fight the new trend. So, Rachel even has a TV in her room now.

Not having had any success with Rachel and Leila, I tried Naomi, but all she said was, "I used to take yoga. Very relaxing." I began to explain that yoga is not an end in itself, but a means to understanding the true nature of illusions, but she had to run to her cheerleading class.

And I haven't been able to reach my best friend

Genevieve, who's living with her Aunt Bernice in Toronto while she trains in a special program for figure skaters and other promising athletes. Every time I call she's either at the rink or asleep, and she hasn't answered my e-mails. She's probably too busy practising or hanging out with her pairs partner, Chris. They love each other but they're waiting until Genevieve's older to go out officially.

Most disappointing of all has been Yoshi's remoteness, reticence, detachment, incuriosity and dispassion. I've written him three e-mails inviting him over, and he still hasn't answered.

I'm starting to seriously worry. It is true that I was once easily swayed. I was clay in Ryan's hands. However, now that I have found spiritual truth, I am no longer a leaf blown to and fro by the wind.

But how can I show Yoshi how I feel about him, if he doesn't come over? I've barely seen him all week. He waved to me from the stairs on Monday, and from the Science lab on Friday. In between those days, he was nowhere to be seen. I guess his responsibilities on the Student Council are weighing him down. I must say I miss our long conversations, our happy times looking at the latest additions to the secret computer game he's designing, and especially the kissing. I hope he can come over this weekend.

The only person who has shown any interest in my quest is Chad, my new friend. Chad is supposed to be in university because he's a genius, but he decided that staying at his grade level was more fun, even if he already knows everything we're being taught. He mostly reads in class, except when he raises his hand to correct the teacher. Our Canadian History teacher, Phyllis, is the only one who hasn't taken Chad's interruptions too well. Phyllis is a jogger who runs to school and comes to class in her running shoes. She says "hello?" at the end of every sentence, and she believes in first names for teachers, because school is our "second home" and teachers are our "second family."

On Monday, when Phyllis said that Canada never invaded Russia, Chad told her, "Actually, Canadian soldiers were part of an expeditionary force sent to fight the Bolsheviks during the civil war that followed the Russian Revolution." Phyllis' face went red and her eyes began to water behind her glasses.

On Tuesday, when she said that Canada never had slaves, Chad raised his hand and said, "Actually, there were 4,092 slaves in Canada by 1759, of which 1,400 were Africans." This time Phyllis had to leave the classroom for a few seconds. When she returned, Chad said kindly, "You were right, Phyllis, about the slaves. There was no slave trade *per se*. People just brought slaves with them." Phyllis seemed eager to change the subject.

On Wednesday Phyllis called in sick, and on Thursday Chad got called into the office at the beginning of class. He was told that from now on he would be taking World History instead of Canadian History. The person teaching World History is "made of sterner stuff" (Shakespeare, *Julius Caesar*).

Anyhow, I told Chad about the Four Noble Truths and the Eightfold Path and the force of karma.

He said, "Schopenhauer took an interest in Buddhism, you know. In a way, it's not surprising, because there really is something depressing about Buddhism. The only way to escape suffering is to pretend you're only half-alive. I'm being deliberately cynical — but it seems to me that Buddhism is so vague on some points that it allows people in the West to justify all kinds of bad behaviour by saying it's Buddhist. Well, maybe that's true for any religion. You can always manipulate religion to serve unethical ends, if you want to. Personally, I agree that you can't have a good life without discipline, but from a psychoanalytic point of view, ascetics are usually neurotic masochists, and from my Western-influenced standpoint, I can't help agreeing. If you ask me, there's a lot to be said for a good movie with someone you love."

Okay, it wasn't the response I'd hoped for, and I have no idea what Chad was talking about, but at least he listened to me.

Meanwhile, Mom is trying to have a "talk" with me, but I've been staying with Dad ever since her news. I don't want to be in her way. I'm sure she has a lot of packing to do.

The only bright spot in my week has been three e-mails from Nigel Sivananda. They are truly gems of wisdom and depth.

In his first e-mail he wrote:

No matter how far a fish swims in the sea, the water is without end. No matter how far a bird flies in the sky, the air is without end. Thus, no creature fails to complete its completeness. Life is the bird and life is the fish. I hope you had a pleasant flight back, my dearest Pauline. I am thinking of you.

The second e-mail was about my mom's plans to abandon me, which I had described to him. He wrote:

Dearest, your mother's love is the moon's reflection in water, the echo of a voice calling, form in a formless world. Those who meditate on the essential as essential and the non-essential as non-essential will attain the essential. You are a child of the universe. Be at peace.

His third e-mail was the deepest of all:

Non-existence cannot be reached through logic. It can only begin at the beginninglessness of the self. This is the wisdom of the Vajrayana. At this moment you are in my arms, in the eternal selflessness of self. Be at peace.

I have memorized these e-mails so that I can learn from their wisdom. They send many tantric thrills up my spine when I think about them.

Now I must get back to the worldly, unfair burden of homework. Ms. Plessix asked us to write an essay this weekend about the two novels we were supposed to read in our "free time." I signed up for *Madame Bovary* and *Anna Karenina*. I finished *Madame Bovary* before Christmas, though I skipped the part with the foot. It was too gross. I also skipped some other sections about politics and other boring topics. As for Madame Bovary's spending habits, I think my mom should read that part, so she can see what happens to wild spenders.

I was going to take *Anna Karenina* with me to London, but it didn't fit into my knapsack. I didn't have much time for reading, anyway.

So I will have to write about *Finnegans Wake*, which Siobhan gave me as a present before I left

London, and which is 300 pages shorter than *Anna Karenina*.

It's not by Finnegan, btw. It's by James Joyce, and it's about someone called Finnegan. I'm not sure what a wake is. Or why there's no apostrophe after "Finnegan." Very confusing — Zane would not approve!

Anyhow, I asked Ms. Plessix if I could write about that novel instead of *Anna Karenina*. She said, "Yes, and good luck to you."

So far I've only read the first page. I'm not sure, but I think it's a description of words going through the mind of someone who is in a coma. Or it could also be a description of planet Earth written by a creature from outer space. It begins: "seashape, in Cain and Abel's, along breadth of sand and pale of port, follows us through a somnium effundo swiftly through to Babel Castle."

Hopefully it will all become clearer in a page or two.

17

Our class rebelled against Ms. Plessix today. She was accused of being unrealistic and overly demanding, and of giving us way, way, way too much work.

She replied bitterly and sarcastically: "Very well, if you want to be as ignorant as the current culture wants you to be, that is fine with me. I was only considering that when I'm old, you'll be the ones making the decisions about what to do with me. How reassuring to know these decisions are being made by people whose intellect has been shaped by car commercials!"

We told her we didn't mind having intellects shaped by car commercials and we promised to favour kind laws for the elderly in the future. As a result, we now only have to write an essay about one novel, and we have a month to get it done. This is a good thing, because *Finnegans Wake* doesn't really get much clearer as you read on. I can see why Zane Burbank III warns writers about books like that. They are far from gripping.

Mom is leaving in a week. Dad told me that she already found someone to move into the condo, as there's a long waiting list for this building. She also finalized the sale of the old, decaying house. Agatone left today, to get his place in Greece ready. It needs curtains.

Mom is still trying to have a "talk" with me but I've been very busy.

To my amazement, Dad asked me how I feel about Mom's desertion. He doesn't usually bring up personal topics.

"Do you mind Mom going away?" he inquired this morning as he was putting logs in the fireplace for a fire. Dad loves fireplaces, and so do I. The only good thing about winter is that we get to have a fire in the living room every day. Dad knows how to move all the sticks around and put in rolled-up newspapers to get a really good fire going. He's quite talented in that area.

I was sitting on the sofa facing the fire and reading a book I found on Dad's shelf. It's called *Siddhartha*! I never noticed it before. It's a profound book about the great Siddhartha, told in a gripping way. The author is Hermann Hesse.

In my opinion, the author of *Finnegans Wake* could pick up a few tips from Hermann Hesse. His book begins: "Where the sun shines on the boats by the bank of the river, there Siddhartha, the handsome son of the Brahman, together with his friend Govinda, grew up, shaded by the house, the Salwood forest and the fig tree. As he swam in the river and performed his sacred rituals, the sun tanned his fair shoulders." This is an excellent beginning. It makes you feel you are right there in the story, and it makes you want to read more about the tanned and handsome son of the Brahman. This is more than I can say for the man in the coma (or the alien).

But back to our conversation. I replied, "Mom can do whatever she wants."

"I'm worried about how this might affect you, Pauline," he remarked. "She's worried, too. She's thinking of cancelling her trip."

"Why should she cancel the trip? I'm not a child," I said haughtily. It's true that Nigel called me a child in his second e-mail, but he only meant it as a metaphor.

Dad went on, "As you know, when I was about your age, my father left us. It was hard on me and Angelo, but even harder for Esmie." Angelo and Esmie are Dad's brother and sister. When Dad was twelve, his father ran away to fulfill his lifelong dream of being a deep-sea diver. He was fascinated by coral reefs.

"That was different," I said. "He didn't stay in touch and he never came back."

"Yes, that was different," Dad agreed. "But I'm still concerned."

"I really don't care, and I have to get back to my book," I announced.

"Mom's been trying to reach you all week. She really wants to talk to you."

"I've been busy," I explained patiently.

"She thinks you're angry at her, and that's why you refuse to see her."

"Dad, I'm trying to concentrate here."

So Dad finally got the message and didn't pursue the conversation.

As for my mom leaving, I'll have one less person to tell me what to do. So it's just as well she won't be here.

I'll miss Agatone, though.

18

I'm still trying to recover from today's events. They were unexpected, from out in left field, like a bolt from the blue, and devastating.

The school dance is tonight. Rachel and Leila are going with Don and Dave, the identical twins. It's going to be Rachel's first dance. I kind of feel bad for her grandmother. There's nothing she can do to stop Rachel, and Rachel's taking advantage of it. On the other hand, why shouldn't she have things other kids have? And Rachel is being kind about it: she's pretending to go to the dance in an old-fashioned prairie dress her grandmother made for her and with her blonde hair in two tight braids. She's going to undo her hair and change into a real dress at Leila's place. "I don't want Gran to have a heart attack," she said.

Naomi, who's in grade ten, is going to the dance with Samir, the school's basketball star. He's very tall. Augusta is going with her secret boyfriend Joel, the coolest guy in the whole school and maybe in all of

Ghent (with Ryan as a close runner-up). His family moved to Ghent from Toronto, but they're originally from Trinidad. Augusta's older sister is going out with Joel's brother Adam, who is also really, really cool, but in an older way. I guess Augusta and her sister have the same taste in guys.

Since Joel is a secret from her parents, Augusta is pretending that she's going alone. Joel is going to arrive later, after her parents drop her off. I never thought Augusta's parents would be so protective. It happened quite suddenly. Before she went out with Ryan, they used to let her do everything. She was allowed to meet artists in cafés in Venice and attend cast parties in London where she chatted with famous actors. She actually exchanged a few words with Helen Mirren.

I wonder what made them change their minds?

Everyone says the school dance is going to be lame, but everyone wants to go. There's nothing else to do in this town in the freezing depths of winter.

Only Chad said he wasn't going, because his boyfriend is still in the closet. The only thing I know about Chad's boyfriend is that he's fourteen, he goes to a private school and he's planning to be a lawyer.

I assumed, naturally, that I would be going with Yoshi.

I was sadly deceived, however. Last night I wrote
Yoshi an e-mail:
Hey, what time do u want to meet for the party?

He wrote back:
*Sorry, Pauline, I was going to tell you, I already made
plans to go with a girl I met, Samantha. I guess this
means we aren't going out any more. I feel we've
grown apart in our interests. I'm sure you'll find someone else to go with.*

In the words of Christina Rossetti, the great poet
of the heart:

*Alas for joy that went before
For joy that dies, for love that dies.
Only my lips still turn to you,
My livid lips that cry, Repent!
Oh weary life, Oh weary Lent,
Oh weary time whose stars are few.*

To put it more simply, I'm shocked and, I have to
admit, puzzled, bewildered and mystified.
I don't understand what happened. Everything was
going so well between us. The evening before I left for
London, we spent three hours finding things on

YouTube. We saw a guy doing Rubik's Cube with one hand in twenty seconds, a guy doing Rubik's Cube with his feet, Einstein the talking parrot and the woman with the dancing dog. We laughed at the comedian doing the Pachelbel rant and were impressed by the boy playing Pachelbel on electric guitar. Yoshi showed me some of his favourite singers. He likes old things: *Russians* by Sting, Sting and Bruce Springsteen singing "The River" and Sinead O'Connor singing "Nothing Compares 2 U" and looking exactly like I feel right now. Little did I know how that song would come back to haunt me.

What made Yoshi change so suddenly? He came to the airport with Dad to pick me up, so he must have still liked me then. It was when he heard about my religious experiences that he became distant.

Maybe Yoshi thinks I'm intruding on his religion. People can be sensitive about things like religion. Or maybe he thinks we are too far apart, now that I have been to London. Or maybe he didn't like the London Underground mouse pad I got him. Or can it be that someone told him something false and untrue about me? I wish he'd let me know, so I can stop guessing. I've realized that guessing makes a person paranoid.

I have no idea what to do about the dance. I have to go. I have to see Samantha, if only to torture myself.

I mean, I have to see what she has that I don't have. If I stay at home alone, I won't be able to bear it. But I can't go by myself, and all my friends are going with dates. I don't want to tag along with them — it'll be bad enough as it is. If only Genevieve were here!

Maybe I'll call Chad. We could go as a platonic couple. I'll try to convince him to dress a little more normally. Chad wears strange, horrible clothes. I thought gay guys were supposed to be good with fashion. On the other hand, geniuses are supposed to be bad with fashion, so maybe the genius part is winning over the gay part. Or maybe that's just Chad's personality. Maybe he likes dressing like a ninety-year-old fisherman.

I wonder who this Samantha is? I know it will hurt me to see her, and I'll probably want to die, but I just can't help being curious.

If Mom were here I could ask her what to do, but she's gone. She left yesterday, and she won't be back for six months. When she came over to say goodbye, I was immersed in the story of Siddhartha, so I just said "Bye" without looking up. I was at a very gripping part of the book.

She didn't get the hint, though. She sat on the sofa and tried to get me to talk to her. I had nothing illuminating to say, however, so she finally gave up.

She left a letter for me, but I haven't opened it yet. I haven't had the time, and I'm not sure where I put it.

19

I sat and wept alway,
Beneath the moon's most shadowy beam.
Watching the blossoms of the May,
Weep leaves into the stream. (CR)

It was a night of tears and despair.

Here are the basic facts:

1. Samantha is the most beautiful girl I have ever seen in my entire life. She is even prettier than Eloise.
2. Samantha is very, very nice.
3. Everyone loves Samantha.
4. Samantha plays soccer, has won singing competitions, has the lead in her jazz ballet show, knows how to break dance and is a chess champion.
5. Samantha is perfect.
6. Samantha's mother is Asian so she has more in common with Yoshi than I do.
7. Samantha is in love with Yoshi.

8. Yoshi is in love with Samantha.
9. They are very, very happy.

I guess I deserve it, because of what happened with Ryan. It was truly short-sighted, slack-witted, injudicious and daft of me to drop Yoshi for someone I barely knew. Now I'm finding out what it feels like.

Knowing I deserve it doesn't make me less sad, though. I'm as sad as I'd be if I didn't deserve it.

Chad did his best to console me. He followed me out of the gym into an empty classroom, which was technically off-limits but no one noticed. There, like the great teacher Siddhartha, I sat and waited for enlightenment to cure me of human suffering. However, you probably need a tree to sit under for enlightenment. All I had to sit under was a poster of our prime ministers.

"Do you want some hiker's mix?" Chad asked me.

I shook my head. "Even my own mother hates me," I mumbled piteously.

"Relationships between parents and children are very complex," Chad reflected. "Take me. My father no longer speaks to me, and he's filled with resentment against me for making him feel ashamed, but he's also terrified I'll die of AIDS one day. As for my mother, she's wracked with guilt. She thinks everything that goes wrong is her fault, and to her, my being gay is another thing that's gone wrong."

"At least you have your boyfriend," I said glumly.

"Yes, that's true. I know how lucky I am. I'm sure he'll be my lifelong partner, so really my father has nothing to worry about. Not that he'd have anything to worry about in any case. I'm not suicidal."

These words made me burst into tears.

"Maybe we should leave," Chad suggested. "I'm not much of a party animal myself."

"Okay. I can't go back in anyhow."

I called Dad and he came to pick us up. He drove Chad home first. Dad didn't ask why I left the dance early. Mom would have been questioning me and Chad non-stop until she got every detail. She likes to know everything.

I went straight to bed, with only Stormy Weather for company. She was purring away on my feet. Life is easy when you're a cat. All you need is food, a cosy house and someone to stroke your fur.

I fell into a troubled sleep, filled with dreams and visions that were "A dagger of the mind, a false creation, Proceeding from the heat-oppressed brain" (Shakespeare, *Macbeth*).

This morning I have a headache, dizziness, nausea and heart irregularity. I don't know how I'll do my homework. Maybe Chad can come over and do it for me. It would take him five minutes.

No e-mail from Nigel today. There was only an e-mail from Mom. She said she arrived safely in Greece and she described the local marketplace. I am really interested in varieties of tomatoes, Mom. Thanks for sharing that.

There was also a letter from Genevieve, finally. I've been trying to reach her for ages without success, and I even phoned her mom to ask if everything was okay. Her mom said that Genevieve was working really hard, but she was fine.

At first I wondered whether she no longer feels that close to me, now that she lives in Toronto. It also crossed my mind that since she's now close to Chris, her figure-skating partner and heartthrob, maybe she doesn't need our friendship any more.

But it turns out I was wrong. She wrote:

sorry sorry sorry Pauline i've been so hard to reach i'm going craaazy here!!!!!!!!!!
i dont know for sure if i'm gonna stick it out i have a new coach, she's unbelievably hard ☹. ttyl i promise.
too bad i missed u at xmas.
I miss u a looooooooooooooooooot.

Phone's ringing, back later.

* * *

(Three stars means "time has passed.")

That was Leila on the phone. She told me that while we were at the dance, Ryan had a party at his house for a few of his friends, and the police were driving casually by when a particular odour caught their attention. That's because Ryan and a few of his friends were out in front smoking pot. Now Ryan's parents are going to have to pay a big fine for possessing marijuana and allowing minors to use it. They thought it was legal in Canada, so they were very surprised.

Leila said one of the top ten finalists from *Canadian Idol* was also at Ryan's party. Ryan's best friend in New York is the son of a big music manager, in case you forgot, and he gave Ryan the phone number.

Leila asked, "Where were you last night, Pauline? I looked for you, but you vanished. Are you going out with Chad now that Yoshi's with that girl?"

"Chad's gay. Where did Yoshi meet her? Where is she from?"

"They met playing soccer, I think. She goes to Ste. Anne's."

"He broke up with me by e-mail! The night before the dance!"

"That's harsh."

"Did you have a good time?" I asked with an unsteady voice.

"Amazing. I think I'm in love. Only I don't know if I'm in love with Don or Dave. I was afraid to ask which one he is. What should I do?"

"I don't feel great, Leila. I have to lie down," I said weakly.

"Okay, talk to you later."

Leila used to be a much more sensitive person.

I lay in bed with a hot-water bottle while Dad made a fire in the living room. When the fire was ready, I moved to the sofa and lay under a blanket with Stormy Weather by my side. She is my only friend.

Dad asked me if I needed anything. I said no. He said Bunny was coming over, was there anything she could bring me? I said no. He said to call him if I needed anything. Then he went upstairs to his studio to paint shoes.

Mom is gone. Yoshi is gone. Genevieve is busy. Dad is busy. Nigel hasn't written in three days. I am failing Math and Science. I do not care.

20

Another e-mail from Mom:

Hi sweetheart,

I haven't heard from you. Did you get my last e-mail? Have you read the letter I left for you? I hope I was able to explain some things to you there. How do you feel about having a brother or sister? I really wanted to talk to you before I left. I miss you terribly. It's so beautiful here. I found a job teaching English. Did you think about the suggestion in my letter? Please write, honey.

Lots of love, Mom.

As to having a step-brother and sister, how can I know how I feel about them if I've never met them? Agatone has three kids altogether: Melody is eighteen, Michail is sixteen and Isaak is fourteen. I've seen photos of them, but you can't tell much from photos.

I've looked around for Mom's letter to see what the "suggestion" is, but I can't find it. It may have been accidentally thrown out. Parenting by correspondence has its consequences.

21

Nigel hasn't answered any of my e-mails since last week. It's been twelve days now without a word. He must have fallen ill. I've written to Daphne and asked her to see whether she can find out what's wrong.

Apart from that I have nothing to report. It is cold out. It gets dark early. School is passing me by in a haze. I'm too weak to chant. Chad tried to tutor me but it was hopeless. He can't make himself stupid enough to tutor me, so I have no idea what he's talking about.

Bunny bought me a statue of the Buddha Siddhartha. I'm too weak, however, to meditate upon his teachings.

Yoshi, why have you deserted me? Nigel Sivananda, why have you not sent me an e-mail?

22

Here is Daphne's letter:

Hello Pauline, dear. So lovely to hear from you. I, too, treasure the memory of your visit to London. It was a true delight seeing you again and getting to know you. You are a unique and thoughtful person, with an open mind and a seeking heart.

As for Nigel, I am afraid he has left the ashram. There seem to have been some problems involving Siobhan and a girl named Eloise. Nigel has gone to visit relatives on the Isle of Wight and he's lying low at the moment. It's possible that he does not have access to a computer. I'm afraid Siobhan and Eloise are both angry with him, though I don't know the details. I'm sure it will all work out, and that he will be in touch with everyone as soon as the air clears.

What are you reading at the moment? How is your novel going? I'm so proud of you, my dear. I miss you already, and can hardly wait to see you again.

Please don't take your mother's departure for Greece to heart. She loves you very much, and it's a sign of her faith in your independence and resourcefulness that she trusts you to manage without her for a few months.

Write any time. Lots of love, your grandmother,
Daphne

First Yoshi, and now this! How much can one poor soul be expected to put up with?

23

I haven't been to school since Daphne's e-mail came.
Dad never questions me if I say I'm sick. He just asks
me if I need anything. He doesn't have Mom's suspicious nature.

Mostly I'm watching movies with Stormy Weather
curled up next to me. Bunny brought me a whole
bunch she thought I'd like, and she was right — they
were very good. They're old movies, but you can't
really tell, apart from the old-fashioned telephones. I
saw *Rain Man* about a man with a secret autistic
brother, *Cat on a Hot Tin Roof* about an alcoholic hus-
band, *High Tide* about an alcoholic mother, *To Kill a
Mockingbird* in black and white, *King of the Hill* about
a boy who is deserted, *The Lotus Eaters* about a girl in
British Columbia, and *Notting Hill* about London —
which was very, very painful to watch. Tomorrow
Bunny's bringing me *Pride and Prejudice*, in six parts.

24

First Bunny had a talk with me. Then Dad.

Bunny has wild, mostly grey hair and she wears velvet-type vests and a lot of handmade jewellery. I can't remember whether I told you that she's extremely rich and likes art. She's making Dad famous. Thanks to her, he's sold all his paintings to various buyers and he's going to have his own show in the spring.

That's not why Dad's going out with her. He's going out with her because he likes her. You can't explain things like that. Not that she's mean, but she's fifty-six. Imagine if the woman in *Notting Hill* was fifty-six years old. The movie wouldn't have made any sense.

Anyhow, Bunny came into my bedroom with tea and delicious oatmeal cookies. She sat on my computer chair and asked, "What's going on, Pauline? How come you've stopped going to school?"

"I'm sick," I whispered faintly.

"You seem to be upset about something."

"Everything is fine," I replied, as the tears flowed down my cheeks. "Genevieve has completely forgotten about me, Mom's in Greece, Yoshi is in love with Samantha, Leila and Rachel are suddenly popular, and Nigel Siv—" but here my voice broke and I was too choked with tears to finish.

"Who's Nigel? Did you meet him in London?"

"He was my guide to Buddhist enlightenment," I wailed forlornly. "I'm lost without him. But he's gone, like all the rest. I shall see him no more."

"What happened?"

"I don't know exactly. Something to do with two girls called Siobhan and Eloise getting mad at him. They don't understand the first thing about enlightenment. They forced him to escape and now he's hiding on the Isle of Wight where they don't have computers."

"Oh dear."

"Yes," I sobbed feebly. "My chakras are gone without him."

"Chakras are always there, you know. They just might be a little on the blink at times."

I was a bit surprised that Bunny knows about chakras. She doesn't look like the type.

"I'll never see him again," I sobbed. "I just know it."

"I can see why you feel so low," Bunny said sympathetically, "but, Pauline, if you miss too much school you'll fall so far behind, you might not be able to catch up."

"Who cares — I'm failing anyhow. I don't understand a single word in Math or Science, and I hate everything else. So what if I drop out? What difference will it make?"

"For one thing, your dad could get into trouble."

"That's just in England," I said. In England they put parents in jail for letting their kids skip. My mom told me that, when she still lived in Ghent. "We don't have jail for kind-hearted parents in Canada," I assured her.

"No, but the authorities do look into it, and it can be unpleasant. I'm sure your dad will be happy to hire tutors to help you out. And I can drive you to an ashram in Toronto if you like."

I shook my head. Enlightenment won't be the same without Nigel.

Bunny sighed and left.

A few minutes later Dad entered the room. He was a lot less sympathetic than Bunny, to say the least.

"Bunny tells me your problems are entirely emotional," he said in an unfriendly, ill-disposed and disaffected voice. "I thought you were really sick."

Even Stormy Weather was put off by Dad's voice. She jumped off the bed and walked away.

"I haven't been feeling well," I whimpered.

"Pauline, I'm disappointed in you. This is the third time in less than a year that you've decided to stop concentrating on school because of some crisis in your life. Believe me, things are going to get a lot harder as the years pass. If you fall apart every time something challenging comes up, you aren't going to have much of a life. Now get out of bed, please, get dressed and let's have some help around the house. The walk needs shovelling, to begin with."

And he left the room.

I was forced to spend the next hour shovelling the snow in the cruel, cold weather, until my back ached and my fingers were frozen stiff.

25

Good news and bad news. The good news is that Genevieve is back. I will be able to tell her about Nigel and Yoshi, who have both abandoned, forsaken and deserted me.

The bad news is that it's because of an injury. She sprained her wrist, so she's off for two weeks. Her mom called me yesterday to tell me she was going to pick up Genevieve in Toronto. I couldn't go with her because it was a school day, and I'm back in school. Dad gave me no choice. He's also hired a tutor called Mr. O'Connor for me. I haven't met Mr. O'Connor yet.

Anyhow, I was really excited about seeing Genevieve, though of course I felt bad about her wrist. But I've missed her so much. And I was feeling worried about her. She didn't sound at all happy in her last e-mail.

She was at home when I got back from school yesterday, and I went straight over to her place. Her house is noisy because she has five brothers, who are all quite hyper. I found Genevieve in her room, her arm in a cast.

As soon as she saw me, she began to cry. Let me explain that Genevieve just about never cries, and I've known her since daycare. Even in daycare she didn't cry. She's just not the type.

So I was quite worried. "What happened?" I asked.

She smiled, embarrassed by her outburst. "Sorry," she said, wiping her tears. "I'm so emotional these days. I'm just tired, I guess." Then she began to cry again.

"Something to do with Chris?"

"Oh no, Chris is awesome. I would have quit altogether if not for Chris. It's just the pressure. It's inhuman." She shook her head and smiled again. "Let's talk tomorrow. These painkillers are making me really sleepy. I'll come over to your dad's after school, so we can have some peace and quiet. I promise I'll be in better shape."

Genevieve was right — she was in better shape today. She came over as soon as I got home and we sat in front of the fire with Stormy Weather purring between us. Stormy Weather loves cuddling up between two people. Whenever two people sit next to each other, her favourite place is right between them. The closer they are, and the more squished she is, the more she likes it.

Genevieve and I had a lot to catch up on. We

devoured an entire plate of Bunny's scrumptious cinnamon raisin buns as we talked. Genevieve was interested in every detail of my trip to London. I told her about Nigel Sivananda and the ashram and Eloise and Siobhan and Nigel's escape to the Isle of Wight. I also told her about Soho and Kew and the London Eye and the mummies and the play. It all seems so long ago and far away now — "It is as a dream, a pleasant dream!" (Jane Austen, *Mansfield Park*.) I told her about Yoshi and Samantha, too.

"What about you?" I probed. "Tell me everything."

"There's nothing to tell. That's just it: it's all so repetitive. You just work like crazy, and then they make you feel you're not working hard enough, and no matter how hard you push yourself they tell you it's not enough, it's not enough, you have to push yourself even more. And now with Bruno gone …"

Bruno was Genevieve's coach from when she first started skating until just a month ago. He's a very jolly person. "What happened?" I asked.

"It's a long story. That's another thing, there's so much fighting and politics. Bruno finally quit. He's back to working privately. And my new coach is a slave driver. She's really good, though, so it's hard to complain. I mean, she knows her stuff, and she's an expert on pairs. Pauline, if not for Chris, I'd leave the program. But I can't let him down."

"You're lucky you have him," I said sadly. "I've been deserted by everyone — even my own mother! I've been so down, but just seeing you makes me feel better."

It's true. It's really strange about talking to a friend. The world can look so gloomy, and then you talk to someone who understands you, and suddenly you feel a ray of hope.

"*Pauvre* Pauline!" (*Pauvre* is French for "poor." Genevieve's bilingual because her parents speak French at home.)

"If only I knew why Yoshi suddenly dropped me. Maybe it's because he met Samantha and realized how much better she was than me."

"You have to talk to him," Genevieve advised.

"What's the point?"

"Do you still like him?"

"I love him!" I cried out in misery.

"Then you have to talk to him and find out what happened. He wouldn't behave so badly without a reason. Even if the talk doesn't get you anywhere, at least you'll know what's on his mind."

"He never tells me what's on his mind. That's our main problem."

"Just force him," Genevieve shrugged. She's more assertive than she used to be, I've noticed.

"How?"

"Well, my mom once gave me a good trick. She said if someone doesn't answer a question, just start counting silently to yourself. By the time you get to fifty, the person almost always says something."

I sighed. "Okay, I'll try. If he agrees to see me, that is. I'll have to find a time when Dad's out of the house, visiting Bunny."

"Have you heard from your mom?"

"She writes now and then," I said in a blasé way. "At least she's marrying someone normal. Remember Griswold?"

At the mention of Griswold we both burst into hysterical laughter and we went on laughing helplessly until our stomachs hurt and our jaws ached. As soon as we began to catch our breaths, one of us would say, "My ankle! My ankle!" and we'd be back where we started. Griswold, in case you haven't read my first novel, was a sad, fake person my mom briefly dated. He had the misfortune of falling off a horse and breaking his ankle when we all went horseback riding.

I'm really, really glad Genevieve is back. Sounds like she needed a break, too. And her wrist injury isn't going to cause any permanent damage, so that's okay.

Raymond seemed happy to see me, too. That's Genevieve's older brother. For once he didn't tease us about believing him, when we were kids, that World War Three had started. In fact, to my enormous surprise, he acted normal. He asked me about London, and said he couldn't wait to go himself. He's saving up for a trip to Europe. He's still goofy, but he's okay. He's exactly my height. We measured back to back.

I've had five letters from Mom this week. They're extremely boring, with detailed descriptions of endless, sandy beaches.

26

Here's the e-mail I wrote to Yoshi:

Hi Yoshi.

I really, really want to talk to you. Maybe you could come over some time when Dad's visiting Bunny. We could sit in front of the fire and eat apple crumble. And we could talk about the past, the present and the future. I hope you can make it because there are many unanswered questions floating in vast, endless space, and why add to them?

Here is Yoshi's answer:

ok

Well, at least he agreed, even if he doesn't sound wildly breathless about it. In school today we decided that he'll come over on Friday after supper. All I have to do is convince Dad to give us some privacy. That shouldn't be a problem. Bunny is always eager to have Dad over.

* * *

I just had the most horrible conversation of my entire life. Not with Yoshi, but with my dad. It was the sort of conversation that makes you want to disappear, vanish into thin air, evaporate, cease to be and leave no trace.

I told Dad about my plans to talk to Yoshi. "I was hoping you could go over to Bunny's so we could have some privacy, Dad," I said, thinking I had a normal father.

"Sorry, Pauline. I'll give you all the privacy you need, but I plan to stay in the house and you're to stay in the living room. I've heard all about London, and how easily you're lured by members of the opposite sex."

Can you imagine? Can you imagine a father saying something like that? To me, his innocent daughter!

Normally, I would have run out of the house, gone to my mom's and never talked to my dad again, until I was at least twenty. But since my mom has deserted me, I'm stuck with my suspicious, faithless and heretical father, and his staggering accusations.

I think I'll save up for a ticket to fly back to Daphne's and live with her permanently. She's the only normal person in my family.

The horror must have shown on my face, because my dad added, "I know you're a good girl, Pauline, but it must be admitted that you can be a bit naïve."

Naïve! That's what my mom wrote about me in a letter to the school when I almost got suspended. (You can read about that unfortunate incident in my second novel.)

"Forget it!" I exclaimed. "Just forget I ever asked. I'll make other arrangements, thank you. I'll go somewhere where I'm appreciated."

And before he had a chance to answer, I stomped out of the room. I couldn't stomp out of the house because we've had more snow and I still haven't cleared the walk, which is my new unpaid job.

The problem with a small town in winter is that there's nowhere to go if you want some privacy. But I suddenly had a very good idea about where we could meet.

My idea has to do with the old, decaying house my mom sold before she left for Greece. When my parents divorced, Mom said she wanted "a fresh start," so Dad stayed in their house and Mom moved into a sprawling, run-down house down the street. "Run-down" is a generous way of describing it. Well, luckily, Bright Homes Realty still hasn't got around to tearing it down. They're probably waiting for the weather to improve.

As it happens, I still have the key. Good thing I haven't cleaned up my room recently. I would have thrown it out.

So I wrote to Yoshi and said:

Change of plans for Friday night. How about we meet at my mom's old place? I still have the key.

Yoshi wrote back:

ok

I hope the electric heaters are still working.

27

I had the talk with Yoshi. It didn't go as well as I'd hoped, to say the least.

It was a lot of work getting organized for the meeting, especially since I had to keep it all a secret from Dad. Luckily, he's lost in his own world most of the time, thinking about how to paint the next shoe. As a result, he doesn't notice a lot of what's going on.

He also doesn't like to intrude. He told me once that he hated the way his own mother asked him a million questions when he was a kid. All day long she'd ask, "Where are you going? What are you doing? Why are you wearing a tie? Why aren't you wearing a tie? Who are you phoning? What did you tell them?" It drove him crazy. So he decided that when he was a parent, he wasn't going to ask a lot of questions.

This can come in handy, especially on a day like today. The first thing I had to do was clear the path in front of the old house. There was a lot of snow piled up between the sidewalk and the front door. So I grabbed our shovel and walked to the old house and started shovelling away.

I worked really hard and it took forever, but people will do a lot for love. Actually, I've become a very experienced snow-shoveller since Dad began forcing me to clear the front walk every time there's the slightest bit of snow.

Once I cleared the path, I had to get my key to work. It wasn't easy, because my fingers were stiff with cold and strain by then, but eventually I managed to open the door.

I thought it might be dusty and spooky inside, but it wasn't. When Agatone first came to visit us from Greece, the plan was for him to live in the old house, so Mom cleaned it from top to bottom. Mom and I were already living in the condo at that point.

Mom also left some things there that she doesn't want any more, like a rug she bought at Zed-Mart, and a lawn table with four matching chairs from Canadian Tire. My mom is a totally irresponsible spender. She has no sense of money.

It was cold in the house, but the heaters were still working, so I turned them all on full blast. Then I went back to Dad's and got a tablecloth, plates, cutlery, the apple crumble (which I had asked Dad to buy at the bakery this morning), milk (Yoshi likes to drink milk with anything sweet) and two glasses. Dad was upstairs, deeply immersed in his art.

I set the table in the old place. It looked quite homey. The only problem was that the house was still really cold. I didn't realize it takes so long for a house to warm up in winter.

So I went back to Dad's and down to our basement and dug out my mom's big quilt. Mom stored some of her things here before she went to Greece. She already had stuff stored in this house from the divorce, and now she has even more. Dad doesn't mind. He never goes into the basement anyhow, except to change Stormy Weather's litter.

Yoshi showed up exactly on time, at seven o'clock. It was still freezing in the house, though.

So we had no choice but to push our lawn chairs together and wrap Mom's quilt around us. It was an auspicious beginning.

"What did you want to talk about?" Yoshi asked in a neutral voice.

"Well, Yoshi, I think there are some feelings that we haven't really shared with each other."

"Such as?"

"Well, I'll start with my feelings. First, I feel very, very, very sad that you've abandoned me for another girl, but, having met her, I can't blame you. She's a million times better than me. Second, I feel a little surprised because it was so sudden. Third, I feel amazed that you could break up with me in an e-mail — but I'm not mad," I added quickly, so as not to ruin the confessional mood. "Fourth, I feel I probably deserve it because of what happened in September when I broke up with you, even though I was sorry after and it wasn't totally my fault because I was tricked by a knave. Fifth, I still have strong feelings for you. Sixth, I'm wondering whether I did something that bothered you. Unless you just got tired of me," I added sadly.

"How could you be tricked by a knave? Were you gambling?" Yoshi seemed confused.

"Gambling? What are you talking about?" Now I was confused.

"You said you were tricked by a Jack."

"Jack? Who's Jack?"

"I'm lost. Weren't you talking about cards?"

"Cards?" I asked. The conversation was getting stranger by the minute.

"You know, King, Queen, Knave."

"I thought it was King, Queen, Jack."

"Jack, or Knave."

"I was talking about Shakespeare's kind of knave. As in bad person."

"Shakespeare? Why Shakespeare?"

"He has a way with words."

"Pauline, that's exactly the problem. I never know where I am with you. I never know what's coming next, Shakespeare or cards or Buddhism or what."

"You mean you're still mad about September?"

"Not really," he said in the same neutral voice. "I figured out what happened there. I mean, everyone knows by now about Ryan. Look what happened with Augusta."

"Augusta? You mean her parents calling his parents?"

"I guess a part of me envies him. He can get any girl he wants, just like that. He just has to look at a girl, and she goes for him. What's his secret? How does he do it? But at the same time, I don't think he should have gone all the way with Augusta, when she's so young. I mean, she acts old, but she's kind of young, in my opinion."

"All the way? You mean sex?"

"Yes, her parents were pretty mad."

"How did her parents find out?"

"I think they caught them at it," he revealed. Yoshi gossiping! Another good sign, I couldn't help feeling.

"He tried to go further than kissing with me, too," I said. "He probably dropped me because I didn't give in."

"I guess he is a bit of a knave," Yoshi smiled, and we both laughed, partly out of embarrassment.

"You don't have to envy Ryan. You have Samantha," I said, pouting a little.

"I'm not going out with Samantha. She doesn't date. She just has friends."

"Really?" I tried to hide my joy at this good news. "But why did you break up with me, Yoshi?" I continued, trying to look stricken, which was somewhat of an effort, now that he'd given me that fabulous news about Samantha, as well as very interesting gossip. "It was so sudden."

"You seem more interested in this Nigel person in London."

"Nigel?! Nigel's my teacher. He's taking me on the path to enlightenment."

Yoshi didn't answer, so I used Genevieve's mom's trick and started counting. I counted to 156 but Yoshi still didn't say anything. That trick doesn't always work, Mrs. Binette.

"There's nothing between me and Nigel," I finally repeated. "He has vanished to the Isle of Wight, anyway. I'll probably never hear from him again."

"Also, Pauline, I'm really not all that interested in Buddhism. I mean, I don't mind if you chant and so on, but you can't expect to drag everyone else into it. And if you meet my family, I'd rather you wouldn't discuss Buddhism with them. They'll think you're insane."

"I thought they were Buddhists, too."

"Not in the same way," Yoshi replied.

"Does that mean you're planning to introduce me to your family, finally?" I asked hopefully. Yoshi has never invited me over to his place because he has some old-fashioned relatives living with him and he's worried they'll think I'm his bride-to-be. He says he'd never have a moment's peace after that.

"I'm just saying, *if* you ever meet them. I don't know when that will be."

"I really want to be together again," I said piteously.

"I don't know, Pauline. I mean what if tomorrow you meet another Ryan, or another Nigel?" Yoshi persisted.

"That's not fair. Nigel was not another person in my life. He was my Buddhist teacher."

"You seemed a lot more interested in his blue eyes than in what the Buddha had to say."

"It's not my fault he has blue eyes!" I protested. I never knew Yoshi was so jealous. He definitely could use some chants for inner peace.

"Pauline, how about we just stay friends for now? We're probably both too young to go steady anyhow."

Friends?! All that shovelling, and getting the apple crumble, and setting everything up in secret — all for nothing! This time I felt as stricken as I must have looked.

"Can't we at least kiss?" I suggested pathetically, snuggling up a little closer. I was hoping that a reminder of our blissful kisses would renew Yoshi's trust in me.

"I really have to go," Yoshi said cruelly, getting up. "My mom wants me to help her find a router."

Arrows of pain pierced my heart, but Yoshi didn't notice. He was too busy calling his mom on his cell and giving her directions so she could pick him up.

We waited in silence for Yoshi's mom. Time stood still. It would be winter forever.

After Yoshi left, long I sat in that cold, dreadful room, "wondering, fearing, doubting, dreaming dreams no mortal ever dared to dream before" (Edgar Allan Poe).

Eventually I bestirred myself. I was afraid Dad would notice that I was out, even though I left the radio on in my room to make it seem I was in there. Also, I needed a tissue. There wasn't even toilet paper in that old house.

Dad never noticed that I was gone, so he was surprised to see me come in, but he didn't say anything. "Yoshi and I went for a walk," I told him, which was true.

He didn't ask for more details. Mom would have wanted to know everything. Good thing she's in Greece.

So that was my day. A day of blighted hope, cruel disappointment and failed expectations. But who can blame Yoshi? Next to Augusta's sophistication, Genevieve's figure skating, Leila's popularity, Rachel's rebelliousness, Ryan's coolness, Chad's genius, Naomi's cheerleading, Eloise's exotic background, Nigel's spirituality and the British people's elegance, I am truly bland.

What is the point of continuing this novel? Zane says novels have to have happy events mixed in with the sorrows. I will spare my readers from reading about sorrow after sorrow, in this endless "winter of our discontent" (Shakespeare, *Richard III*).

28

I'm continuing with this novel after all, because something very unexpected has happened. I may be a witness in a murder investigation! A dead man was found in Mom's old house.

At first I thought I'd be in huge trouble. Two police officers came over to talk to me and Dad. One was a large, muscular woman with unusually green eyes and the other was a small, thin man with freckles. Once you had to be tall to be a police officer, but short people complained, so they lowered the height requirement and now you can be as short as Agatone and still join the police force.

Anyhow, the two officers told us that someone had been in the old house recently, and this person had shovelled a path to the door, and had entered the house with a key, and had apparently eaten apple cake there, possibly with another person.

"What's this all about?" Dad asked.

"Would you happen to have the key to that house, Mr. Carelli?"

"I don't, no." My dad looked at me.

The police officers looked at me.

There is no point trying to hide from the police. They can take your fingerprints, or even a strand of hair, and prove it was you.

"It was me," I mumbled. I was kind of glad the police were there, as Dad couldn't get too mad at me in front of them. They'd arrest him for child abuse.

"Can you tell us when you were there?" the woman officer asked. She had quite a soft voice, for a police officer.

"Friday, between about seven and eight. I'm sorry. I just figured no one was using it, and I wasn't sure if my mom still owned it or not." That lie just slipped out.

"Did you see anything unusual?"

"No, it was just the way Mom left it."

"Were you with anyone?"

"Yes, with my friend Yoshi."

"Well, a body's been found there."

"I'm innocent!" I cried out.

"We think it's a case of a homeless man looking for shelter," the other officer reassured me. "He must have seen the path, and tried the door. You left it unlocked."

"Oh, yeah," I mumbled. "I forgot."

"But we have to wait for the coroner's initial report. We'll be in touch if we have any more questions."

Then they left. I thought Dad was going to get really angry, but he's unpredictable. All he said was, "Sad, to die alone in an empty house in winter."

That was it.

What if there's really been a murder? Will I be a suspect? Will I have to go to a courtroom and give evidence?

29

It turns out I know the man who died, and so does Yoshi. He was in a play the two of us saw last year, *Phantom of the Opera*, which was put on by Women for People Who Have Less. The man who died played the phantom. He wasn't bad, either. I found out from the newspaper that he used to be a singer, so that explains it. He even made a record a long time ago, before things started going wrong for him and he became a Person Who Has Less and stopped cutting his fingernails.

I feel terrible. At first I thought it was my fault he died, because I didn't lock the door of the old house. I thought that maybe if he hadn't been able to get in, he would have collapsed on the street and maybe someone would have seen him and called an ambulance.

But then I found out that he was dying of cancer anyhow, and nothing could have saved him. At least he died indoors. Still, Dad's right, it's really sad that he died alone in the cold. Some people have no luck at all.

I have a few other things to report. First, I looked up the Isle of Wight on the internet. They definitely have computers there. It's a modern island, with night-clubs, restaurants and tourist attractions. I'm sure they have an internet café.

So, just in case Nigel decides to take a break from meditating, and check his e-mail, I sent him a letter:

Hi Nigel,

I heard from Daphne that you are on the Isle of Wight. I checked it out on the internet and it looks charming indeed. I hope you are enjoying the "wealth of footpaths, home to many unique flowers and fauna." It must be gratifying to meditate in such peaceful surroundings. I'm trying to meditate, too, but it's hard without any word from my spiritual teacher, so I hope you will find a computer somewhere on the island and send me a letter.

Waiting for further enlightenment,
your devoted student,
Pauline

The second thing I have to tell you about is my conversation with Genevieve. It's a bit personal, but Zane says to *reveal hidden truths*, and that means revealing things even if they're embarrassing. However, if you are shy or underage, please skip this part.

Genevieve's been coming over every day. She's feeling restless at home. She brought schoolwork that she's supposed to be doing, but school was never at the top of Genevieve's list of Reasons to Live. School is at the very bottom of that list.

I told Genevieve how Yoshi broke my heart. "When I suggested we kiss, he remembered he had to help his mom find a router!"

"That sucks," Genevieve agreed.

"I have to find a way to get him to trust me again," I said with steely determination. However, my steely determination almost immediately gave way to quivering doubts. "Do you think it's hopeless?" I whimpered.

"Remember what Mr. Pete said?" Genevieve replied, referring to our teacher last year. To Genevieve, Mr. Pete was the embodiment of human perfection. "He said some things are easy and some things are hard, but everything is achievable."

"If only I had Augusta's confidence!" I lamented. "She can have anyone she wants."

"I wonder why she gave in to Ryan," Genevieve mused.

"Well, he's cute. And he makes you feel important. And he makes you feel you're really special — you know, different. Like the two of you are different from everyone else. And he makes you feel he really, really likes you. Plus, he's cute."

"Well, how did *you* resist him?" Genevieve wanted to know.

"In my case, it wasn't hard," I told her. "I'm not ready to be seen — you know — without clothes," I explained, lowering my voice. "I'd rather die. The guy would burst out laughing if he saw me. I don't have boobs, and also ... also ..." I began to cough and clear my throat so that I wouldn't have to finish the sentence. Even with your best friend, some things are impossible to say.

"Maybe I'm abnormal." I was suddenly worried. "I'm fifteen already. What if I never look normal?"

"Oh, don't worry," Genevieve said calmly. "Whatever's supposed to happen will happen sooner or later."

"Anyhow," I continued, "I think sex should be a deeply spiritual experience. Ryan is cute, but he's not a deeply spiritual person. Augusta didn't even like him all that much. That's the part I don't get."

"Maybe she was curious," Genevieve said, and her eyes got misty. "I miss Chris," she sighed. "It's hard to skate with someone you love, and then watch him pack up his skates at the end of the practice session and go home. But he says we have to wait at least another year to go out. I will die waiting."

"Well, at least you get to skate together ... You know, I think I figured it out, just now. I think Augusta did it to get power," I speculated. "You know what Augusta's like. She needs to be in power. If she does it with someone she doesn't like, she keeps the power. Because she proves that she doesn't care one way or another."

"That's crazy," Genevieve laughed.

"We're all bound by illusions and desire," I explained. "We must distinguish the essential from the non-essential in order to achieve the path to purification."

"That reminds me," Genevieve stood up abruptly. "I promised my parents I'd go to mass today. I should get a move on."

"Will you confess?" I asked. Only last week I saw a confession scene on this supernatural police show on TV. A man confessed to murder in the confessional booth, and the whole church began to quake. Then terrorists burst in and kidnapped a little boy in a coma. It was quite gripping.

Genevieve laughed again. "What would I confess? I'm perfect! Anyhow, my parents think confession is old-fashioned. They just want us to grow up with some religion, in case we ever have hard times. I'll call you tonight."

I'm really going to miss Genevieve when she goes back to Toronto.

The third thing I have to tell you about is my mom's "suggestion." In case you forgot, my mom asked me in one of her e-mails what I thought of her "suggestion." I still haven't found the letter she left me before she went to Greece, so I didn't know what the "suggestion" was. I finally remembered to ask Dad.

"Do you know what Mom suggested in her letter?" I casually asked him at dinnertime. We were having pizza, for a change. Unless Bunny cooks us something, we usually have either pizza or spaghetti. Dad could eat the same thing for years and not get bored, or even notice. "I seem to have misplaced the letter."

"You didn't read her letter?" Dad seemed surprised, but he didn't pry. "Well, she suggested you visit her during the spring break. That's all."

"No way," I said with decisiveness, certainty and "the dauntless spirit of resolution" (Shakespeare, *King John*).

"How come?" Dad asked.

"First, we're going to be loaded down with homework. Second, it's too expensive. Third, a week isn't enough to travel to Greece and back. Fourth, I have no interest whatsoever in Greece or in markets."

Dad nodded. He didn't seem to have an opinion one way or another.

"Mom is a real spendthrift," I commented. "She should read what happened to Madame Bovary."

"I'm sure she's managing." Dad didn't seem at all worried. That's because he hasn't seen her credit card bills. "Well, if you're not interested in going to Greece, Mom might come here to see you."

"Tell her not to!" I said. "It's a complete waste of money. I'll be way, way too busy to see her."

"Why don't you tell her yourself?" Dad suggested. He was right, it was safest to tell her myself. I went to the computer and wrote,

Hi Mom,

Dad says you are thinking of coming for a visit during spring break. Don't come, Mom! I'm going to be way, way too busy to see you, so if that's the reason you're coming it's a complete waste of money. Have a good time at the market.

The last thing I have to tell you about is Mr. O'Connor, my tutor. He's extremely nice. He runs a youth group at one of the churches around here, and I must say I can see why youths would join that group, even if it's in a church. He's around Dad's age, but he's much more understanding. We had a long talk about Buddhism. I found him quite well-informed.

He's also quite critical, for a churchy guy. "This is a terrible math curriculum," he said, shaking his head, "but I'll try to make it as painless as possible."

I asked him why it was a bad curriculum. His answer was a bit on the insulting side. He said, "They want to teach you to think mathematically, instead of giving you basic math skills. But only one in ten students can think mathematically, and it's not something you can teach. The problem is that the people drawing up the curriculum are themselves mathematicians. They refuse to accept reality."

I guess I'm not one of those rare students who can think mathematically. "I'm writing my third novel," I told him, to show him that at least I have talent in something.

"I'd love to ask you more about it, but your dad is paying me by the hour, so we had better get some work done."

We worked for two hours. Mr. O'Connor sighed frequently. Before he left, I heard him tell Dad, "The road is long but at least they sell popcorn on the way." That was supposed to be a joke. He has his own sense of humour.

Those are the things I had to tell you about. I know Zane says not to jump from topic to topic, but I didn't have a choice in this chapter.

30

Genevieve has gone back to Toronto, three days early. She was impatient to get back, because of Chris. I really miss the days when she lived here full-time, and Rachel made tablecloths on her grandmother's loom, and Leila wasn't obsessed with Don and/or Dave. I even miss Augusta hanging out with all of us. Those days are gone forever. Genevieve is no longer here, Rachel is a rebel, Leila is popular and Augusta is out of our league now. She has experience.

I'm in a deep state of ennui these days. Mr. Pete, our teacher last year, taught us about ennui. It is a feeling of hopelessness and desolation brought on by the realization that life is meaningless and basically sucks.

Even the good mark I got on my *Madame Bovary* essay failed to bring me out of "spirit's melancholy and eternity's despair" (Elizabeth Barrett Browning). My essay was called "G. Flaubert as a Novelist: His Style and Strong Points." Ms. Plessix wrote:

Your focus on literary technique was refreshing, Pauline. You may be interested in taking a look at Desire in Language: A Semiotic Approach to Literature and Art *by Julia Kristeva, translated by Alice A. Jardine, Columbia University Press, 1982.*

I looked for that book at the Ghent Public Library but they didn't have it. Instead, I took out a book called *A Writer's Diary* that caught my eye. The writer keeping the diary is Virginia Woolf. That's a catchy name for an author. Zane would definitely approve.

31

Today was Sunday. I thought I'd stay in bed all day, but Chad called at ten in the morning and asked if he could come over.

It was his first time at our place. I showed him Dad's studio, and he looked at all the paintings of shoes and boots on roads. "A sort of play on surrealism," he commented. "The result is funny and moving. I didn't realize your father was such a good artist."

I wasn't in the mood for talking about my father or his art. We went back downstairs and sat at the dining room table, feasting on Bunny's leftovers. Chad ate voraciously.

"I need advice," he said, helping himself to a generous portion of potato salad.

"Okay," I replied.

"The thing is, I'm getting desperately bored in school. I know I should be in university, but I don't want to leave ... my friend."

"Your friend in the private school?"

"Yup. That's why I stayed in the first place. I did apply to a few universities, but I didn't want to spend so much time apart from him."

"Don't his parents suspect anything?"

"No, we're discreet. The thing is, I'm starting to feel claustrophobic in school. I'm becoming quite neurotic, in fact. And I think if I were in a more appropriate environment, I'd be more myself."

"Genevieve left me to go to Toronto," I said. "Of course, it's not exactly the same. We're just best friends. Still, she went to Toronto because it was better for her career, and in the long run it'll be better for our friendship, too. I really miss her. Everything's gone wrong since she left." I spread garlic butter on a slice of French bread and bit into it, to ease the pain of memory.

"That's what worries me. My friend might not do well if I left."

"Can't you go to a university nearby?"

"Yes, but I'd still have to live on campus, and I'd only be able to come in to Ghent on weekends. And for once in my life I'd be bogged down with work. It would become increasingly complicated to arrange trysts."

"I can't imagine you with a guy, Chad. You're so …

young. And you dress weird. You dress like a loner."

Chad laughed. "Everyone complains about my clothes. We live in a pathologically sartorially obsessed society. As for my age, the problem for someone like me, Pauline, is that I don't feel young."

"Sar-what?"

"Sartorially. That means related to clothes."

"Good word."

"I agree."

"Chad, can I ask you something? Do you wake up every morning thinking, 'I'm a genius'?"

"No, I wake up every morning thinking, 'When am I going to see Clyve today?' Now I've given away his name. You have to promise not to tell anyone."

Clyve! That's the name of the guy Augusta invited to her post-New Year's Eve party last year. It must be the same Clyve. How many Clyves can there be who go to private school?

On the other hand, maybe with a name like Clyve you have no choice but to go to private school.

"I think I know him — wasn't he the guy hanging out with Augusta? But don't worry," I quickly added, "I wouldn't tell a soul, of course."

"Yes, that's him. It's his parents," Chad sighed. "They wouldn't take it well. They have very different plans for him."

"Is that why he acted like he was interested in Augusta?"

"Oh, Augusta knows. She was just trying to help him."

I told you Augusta has a generous side!

"Well, can't you go to university part-time?" I suggested.

"If I'm not full-time I can forget about the scholarships they offered me, and I wouldn't be able to commute anyhow. No, I'd have to enrol full-time."

"If it's any help at all, I can deliver letters to Clyve secretly."

"That's kind of you to offer, Pauline. Luckily, there's e-mail."

"I think you should go, Chad. That's the advice I gave Genevieve. It's important to pursue your dream."

"The problem is I have more than one dream at the moment," Chad said. "This potato salad is yummy. Invite me over more often, Pauline."

Dad came downstairs at that point. He was wearing his work clothes, which are jeans and a T-shirt covered with paint. He didn't look very presentable.

"Hi, Chad," Dad said brightly. He seemed to be in a very good mood.

"Hi, Mr. Carelli. I saw some of your work upstairs — I really like it. I hope we're not stealing your lunch."

"Not at all. I stuffed myself last night, I need a break today. Pauline, Bunny and I discussed marriage last night. We'd still have our two homes, so nothing would change radically for you. It would only mean seeing a little more of Bunny than you do now. Anyone want tea?"

32

I have accepted Dad's marriage plans. I think he's looking for companionship. He probably isn't the type who can be happy all on his own. There's nothing wrong with companionship between people. Dad said he and Bunny aren't selling their houses or moving in together, which means that he intends to continue having the same casual friendship with Bunny as before. There is a comfortable sofa bed up in the studio for when she sleeps over.

Of course, it will be disappointing for Bunny, as it's obvious that she is madly in love with Dad and would like to have an intimate relationship with him. She is constantly touching his arm and sitting close to him. However, she will have to accept the realities of age.

If only I could talk to Yoshi about all this! He'd understand all the angles. Even Mom would be a good person to talk to about this particular subject. But all I could do was text Genevieve: HI GF PCM ASAP I ND 2 TLK2U XOX.

I'm afraid I have nothing more to say.

33

An e-mail arrived from Nigel:

Hey Pauline. Fabulous to hear from you. How are you doing, my love? Alas, penury has forced me to leave the ashram. I'm presently working at my cousin's bike and motorbike repair shop. These are the fruits of long years of toil in the hallowed halls of Oxford — one gets to repair tyre punctures. I am considering my future options and have applied for a teaching job in Korea. Perhaps something will come of it.

I'm afraid I am no longer as deeply immersed in Eastern philosophy as I was, and I have changed my name back to Nigel Thorne. Valuable as those spiritual insights may be, they are often misunderstood in this part of the world. At least I have not incurred your ire, dearest Pauline. That is because your soul is pure. May we meet again some time in the future when you are of age.

Take care, Nigel (Thorne)

In case you don't know what some of those words mean, here are a few explanations, which I got from my dad: "Penury" means poverty. "Hallowed" means holy or important. "Oxford" means Oxford University. "Tyre punctures" means flat tires. "Incurred your ire" means made you mad.

Poor Nigel! Forced by poverty to give up on the path to enlightenment.

Meanwhile, I'm clinging to the few feeble rays of hope in this letter. There are definitely computers in Korea, if he ends up there. On the other hand, what will we talk about, now that he can no longer be my spiritual guide?

Another glimmer of hope has appeared inside the dark cave of my life. Leila phoned and suggested a triple date: her and Rachel with Dave and Don, and me with Yoshi. She wants to go to this new place they're opening in a town nearby. It's some sort of big mall with a Cineplex and restaurants and fountains. She says her mom will drive us there in their van (which means a lecture on flossing the entire way) and she asked if Dad can pick us up when we're ready to go home.

Apparently Yoshi has already agreed! This is encouraging news, indeed. Maybe he's thought it over and has realized that we are meant for each other. Maybe he's remembered the walks in the bird sanctuary, our identical feelings about pencil shavings, how enthusiastically I admired the secret computer game he's designing. Maybe I will once again feel his heavenly lips touching mine!

I asked Dad about giving us all a lift home, and he said no problem. He'll spend the evening at Bunny's and pick us up on the way home. Bunny lives around that area, too, in her big mansion.

Oh Yoshi, Yoshi! Will you come back to me in the new mall?

34

Oh mall, oh sweet, oh lovely mall! I shall never forget what befell me within your walkways.

We all met at Leila's house. I got into the van first and sat in the back corner. Yoshi got in right after me — and sat next to me. This was already a good sign, though I didn't want to get my hopes up too high. Since Don and Dave were officially Leila's and Rachel's dates, Yoshi had no choice but to sit next to me.

Leila's mother didn't talk about flossing, for a change. Her topic this time was posture. She can't believe how poor the posture of teenagers has become. She says it's because of computers.

"If you kids don't start doing yoga or some sort of stretching, you're no longer going to look like *Homo erectus*," Leila's mother said.

Instead of dying when her mother said that, Leila shrieked with hysterical laughter, which made everyone else laugh. Soon they were all cracking jokes about Neanderthalus Computerus.

I kept wanting to reach out for Yoshi's hand, but I controlled myself. If someone rejects you, it's suicidal to try a second time.

Finally we reached the mall. It was huge. You could actually get lost in that mall, unlike ours, where there are only two directions you can go in: up the strip towards Sears or down the strip towards Zed-Mart.

We were all starving, so we went to this Italian eatery where you watch them make the pasta in these big vats of boiling water. Everyone got excited about that. Canadians will get excited about anything. It's because we don't get out much all winter long.

I had tortellini. It was delicious, and I was starting to feel a little better. I even began to participate in the conversation. Don (or Dave) was talking to Leila about soccer, and Dave (or Don) was talking to Rachel about her religion and all the rules she was breaking in one night.

I said, "The good thing about Buddhism is that there aren't any rules like 'no TV' or 'no toasters' or 'dress modestly.' All you have to do is understand the Four Noble Truths: life is suffering; suffering is a result of attachment; you can stop suffering by detaching yourself from earthly desire; there is an eightfold path to achieving this goal."

At first there was a brief silence. I thought they were all trying to digest the deep wisdom of Siddhartha. But I was sadly mistaken. Leila said, "You know, Pauline, you used to be fun to be with. Now all you do is talk about depressing things no one has heard about or has the slightest interest in."

I was speechless, dumbfounded and flabbergasted, especially when no one contradicted her.

Dave, if it was him, agreed with Leila. "You should try to lighten up," he advised me. "Like the song says, 'Don't worry, be happy.'"

Don said, "Be happy, don't worry."

Rachel said, "Maybe you should make an appointment to see Miss Mordant at school."

Yoshi was noticeably silent during their heartless attack.

I blurted out, "How can I be happy when Yoshi has broken my heart!" And I burst into heart-wrenching tears and ran from the table.

I stopped at a fountain of multi-coloured lights. Water sprayed out in a dreamlike display of pink, blue and green shades. I watched innocent children throwing pennies into the fountain.

Suddenly — I'm still trembling at the memory — I felt a hand on my shoulder. It was Yoshi.

No words were spoken. We knew each other's

hearts. We looked long and deep into one another's eyes. "Did you find a router?" I finally asked.

Yoshi laughed. "Yes, and it was even on sale," he said.

We held hands as we walked back to the table. We held hands right through the movie we all went to see after our meal. The movie was hilarious. It was called *The Clone of Maplewood Heights*. In case you haven't heard of it, it's a comedy about this really cute clone who's sent by the U.S. government to a suburban high school. He's been cloned to be hugely popular and to make everyone sign up for the army. It was a biting satire.

We all liked the movie. Don and Dave laughed in a loud, exhibitionistic way. Leila snorted every time she laughed, which made everyone around her laugh even harder. Yoshi chuckled, and I smiled blissfully.

After the movie Rachel had her ears pierced, Don and Dave bought long strings of liquorice and pretended they were snakes, and finally my dad picked us up in his truck.

Yoshi is coming over tomorrow. I will be counting the minutes.

35

Oh, I am fainting, I am fainting! Today a letter came from Floating Raft Books! They want to publish my books!!!!!!!!!!!!!!!!!!!!!!!!!

I sent them my first two novels just before the holidays. I carefully followed the instructions in Zane's chapter, "Getting Published." His advice was obviously excellent, since today I received this letter:

Dear Ms. Carelli-Bloom,

Thank you for sending us your two novels. We were all falling off our chairs as we read them. We are interested in discussing publication terms. Would you be so good as to contact us at your earliest convenience? As we are a small press, we cannot offer an advance, but we would do our best for your books.

Sincerely,

Billie Rockwell, Editor

I almost stopped breathing when I read that letter. They were so excited by my novels they fell off their chairs!! I ran upstairs to where Dad was painting. He hates to be interrupted. "Just a minute," he said in an annoyed voice. He was deeply absorbed in his latest painting of a loafer.

Finally he said, "What is it, Pauline?"

I was too excited to speak, so I thrust the letter in his hand and he read it.

He frowned, reread it, and then said, "It's just some scam, Pauline. You mustn't fall for these gimmicks."

"But it's from Floating Raft Books, Dad. It says so on the letterhead."

"I never heard of them. I'm sure it's a practical joke. Let's go downstairs, I need a cup of Cofmalt."

"Dad, it can't be a practical joke," I pointed out, following him downstairs to the kitchen. "I sent them my novels, and no one else knew about it."

"They just want your money, Pauline. Remember that poetry scam? They tell you your poem won a prize, and then they ask for sixty dollars to print out a desktop booklet with your poem in it — along with the poems of all the other people who got taken in."

I admit that I started feeling a little doubtful. I know Dad's right about those poetry scams, because I once almost fell for one myself. I entered a poetry competition, and I got a letter telling me I was the lucky winner. I was seven years old at the time, so that sort of gave it away. I still remember the poem I sent in:

Why do people cry?
Why Why Why?
Why do things have to die?
Why Why Why?
Why do parents fight?
Why Why Why?
Why don't I have a cat?
Why Why Why?

My parents were forced to tell me that the whole thing was just a fraud. I did get Stormy Weather as a result of that poem, though, so it wasn't a total loss.

"Why don't we do a search on the internet?" Dad suggested. He went to my computer and typed in "Floating Raft Books." A website came up right away. "Hmm," he muttered. "It says here they're located in Cereal, Alberta. Let's see if there's such a place."

I never knew Dad was so suspicious. On the other hand, Cereal *is* a somewhat unusual name.

But Cereal is a real place. Dad looked it up on the internet and found that it is "a closely-knit community offering hometown appeal, quiet streets and affordable housing." They have to be close-knit, as they only have

160 people. They used to have 200 but forty left. They have two attractions: a seven-foot antelope statue, and a museum about "times that were both simpler and desperate." Can you imagine being a teenager in Cereal? I'd say times would still be pretty desperate for them.

The website showed all the books published by Floating Raft, with pictures of the covers. It was an impressive list indeed. Apart from nine volumes of poetry by famous Canadian poets, they have published three novels: *Caesar's Toga* by Samantha Halliweather, *Faulkner's Walking Stick* by L. Chu and *Michelangelo's Towel* by Cendrée d'Aizy. (Unlike James Joyce, they remembered to put in the apostrophes in their titles.)

"Well, it doesn't appear to be a scam," Dad admitted. "They're supported by the Canada Council."

"Dad, why is it so hard for you to believe that someone wants to publish my novels? I worked really hard on them, and I followed all the rules in Zane Burbank III's book."

"Pauline, let's not jump to any conclusions. We still don't know what the offer is, and whether it's serious. It's possible that they're only interested in the idea, not in the books themselves."

"I'm really, really insulted, Dad, that you can't believe anyone would want to publish my books."

"I just don't want you to be disappointed, Pauline. Maybe I could read what you sent them? That will give me a better idea of what's going on."

I hadn't thought of my parents reading my novels. I mean, there's a lot about them in my books, because Zane's First Rule is: *Write about what you know.* But if I'm going to be published, my parents will have to read what I wrote about them. If they don't like it, they should think twice about how they behave in the future.

So I opened the file called "My First Novel," and Dad sat down at my desk and began to read. Soon he was making choking, coughing and spluttering noises, and his eyes were getting kind of watery. My novel had clearly moved him.

He only read three or four pages. He took a few minutes to compose himself, and then he said, "Pauline, I'll print out the rest and read it later tonight. And I'll phone your mom and see what she thinks. I'll also call Floating Raft Books, with your permission."

"Sure, Dad," I said. Good news makes people easygoing, I've noticed.

If you're planning to write a novel, you should definitely buy Zane's book. It will bring you great fame and fortune.

It will be quite hectic, being famous. Everywhere I go, people will swarm to get my signature, and newspapers will call me to ask for my opinion. Photographers will pop out of bushes to catch me as I walk to the corner store. I will be interviewed on television, under the glaring lights of the cameras. Maybe I'll even get to meet Oprah.

Now I have to call Yoshi, Genevieve, Leila, Rachel, Augusta, Naomi and Chad, and tell them the news.

36

Dad spoke to Mom, and to Floating Raft Books, and they have sent me a contract by e-mail. I printed it out, and Dad said it looks fine, so we signed it. Dad had to sign along with me because I'm under eighteen. The contract was seven pages long. I never realized it was so complicated to publish a book.

I asked Dad, "Do you mind being in a novel that millions will read?"

He replied, "I don't think there's anything *too* defaming in it." "Defaming" means that it's bad for your reputation.

My only other news, which is almost as exciting, is that I'm *finally* going to meet Yoshi's parents. He invited me over to his place this weekend.

I must say, a lot has happened to me in a very short time:

1. Dad is getting married.
2. Mom's in Greece and she's getting married, too.
3. I visited the great city of London.

4. Nigel taught me the ways of Siddhartha.
5. I'm getting published!
6. Yoshi and I broke up and made up.

One more thing: Mom's having a baby. I think I forgot to mention that. She told me about it in the missing letter, the one I never read. This morning Bunny asked me how I felt about Mom having a baby, and that's how I found out.

So it looks like I will have a half-sister or half-brother. I guess I'm happy about it. I don't know whether Mom will want to come back to Ontario. She seems quite taken with the beaches and markets of Greece. So I may have to travel to Greece after all.

I don't think this book can hold any more information. Zane says, *Do not overload your novel with too many events and changes.* So I will end this novel here, especially since my life is going to change a lot, now that I'm going to be a famous author.

Besides, Mr. O'Connor says I need to spend more time on my schoolwork and less time on the computer.

I still have to think of a title for this book. Zane says titles have to be gripping and mysterious. Maybe I'll call this novel *The Secret Journey of Pauline Siddhartha.* I like that name, Siddhartha — it's extremely exotic. "Secret" is for the mysterious part of the title. And "Journey" is what my story is all about, because the great teacher Siddhartha taught me that life is change, and you have to go along with the great current of existence.

Now I just need a quote for the ending. How about one last contribution by Christina Rossetti, a truly accomplished poet:

All things that pass
Are Wisdom's looking-glass.

See you later!

☺

This is where it all began!
Pauline, btw
BOOK ONE:

"Yoshi, I have something I want to ask you." (Zane says it's good to start a chapter with a quote, before you tell the story.)

We had finally found a safe place to go to together. We went to see a production of *Phantom of the Opera* put on by Women for People Who Have Less. A few People Who Have Less were going to act in the play and all the money was going to a shelter in Toronto.

We figured we wouldn't run into anyone there because (a) it was in another town and (b) no one knew about it. The only reason I got to hear about the play was because several of my mom's ex-convict clients were helping out.

It was one of our warmest days this year. You could feel in the air that spring's coming soon. Mom gave us a lift. Her car's back from the garage, but the mechanic says it "isn't long for this world." He's in the Ghent Evangelical Choir, so he has a poetic way of putting things.

As we were driving there, I decided I was going to confront Yoshi about why we never go to his place.

So when we were in the lobby of this tiny theatre, waiting to be let in, I told Yoshi I had to ask him something.

There wasn't an immense crowd, as you can imagine.

"What is it?" Yoshi asked nervously.

"How come you never ask me over to your place?"

"How come you never ask me over to your mother's place?" he tried to distract me.

"I told you why." (I did.) "My mom's house is lopsided, run-down and embarrassing."

Yoshi didn't say anything.

"So?"

He coughed and looked at his shoes.

I insisted. "Don't you think if we're going to be friends you have to trust me? Do you have werewolves living with you?"

He nodded.

"Very funny," I said.

"Well, not werewolves, but my … my family."

"Your family?"

Just then a Man Who Has Less, and who also has the longest and yellowest fingernails I've ever seen in my life, opened the door, so we had to stop talking and take our seats.

The play was pretty bad. Everyone sang off-key, the set fell down twice, the Man Who Has Less (who also played the Phantom) had two coughing fits, and a woman behind us kept saying over and over, "I saw this on *Broadway*." I wanted to strangle her …

At intermission, I urged Yoshi to continue.

He sighed. "Aside from my parents, I live with my great-aunt, my uncle, my great-cousin and my grandmother," he said gloomily.

"What's a great-cousin?" I asked.

"I have no idea."

"So, what's the problem?"

"Well, they're very old-fashioned," he said darkly. "Especially my older relatives. If I bring you home, they'll just assume that …" he blushed.

"That I'm your future wife?" I guessed.

"Uh-huh. And I'll never hear the end of it. Have I inspected your family? Do you have an unblemished background? Do you have a dowry? A dowry, for God's sake."

"What's a dowry?" I asked.

"That's money or stuff you bring into the marriage with you," he mumbled.

Poor Yoshi! At least when I was tormented at school I could count on not having my privacy invaded at home. But Yoshi would be getting it from both ends.

"I see your problem," I said. "But couldn't you just explain?"

Yoshi only sighed more deeply.

My mom picked us up after the play was over and then we picked up Bernard and the four of us went out for dinner, except that Yoshi and I sat at a separate table.

I warned my mom that if she gave any indication that she and Bernard are more than business-like acquaintances, I'd move into my dad's for good and she would never, ever see me again.

She said okay, and I admit she kept her promise. Still, it was sort of annoying having her and that crazy Bernard with us. But we had no choice. We're too young to drive.

I've decided that Yoshi is definitely my type.

AUTHOR PHOTO: UZI WITKOWSKI

Edeet Ravel was born on an Israeli kibbutz and grew up in Montreal. She is the author of four award-winning novels, including *Ten Thousand Lovers*, which was a finalist for the Governor General's Award, and *A Wall of Light*, winner of the Canadian Jewish Book Award and a finalist for the Giller Prize and Canada/Caribbean Commonwealth Prize. Edeet also works as a peace activist and was a teacher for two decades. She lives in Guelph with her daughter Larissa.

By printing

The Secret Journey of

Pauline
Siddartha

on paper made from 100% recycled fibre (40% post-consumer recycled) rather than virgin tree fibre, Raincoast Books has made the following ecological savings:

- 25 trees
- 2,380 kilograms of greenhouse gases (equivalent to driving an average North American car for five months)
- 20 million BTUs (equivalent to the power consumption of a North American home for three months)
- 14,581 litres of water (equivalent to nearly one Olympic sized pool)
- 890 kilograms of solid waste (equivalent to nearly one garbage truck load)

(Environmental savings were estimated by Markets Initiative using the Environmental Defense Paper Calculator. For more information, visit www.papercalculator.org.)